RODDY DO

Roddy Doyle was born in Dublin in 1958. He is
the author of eleven acclaimed novels including
The Commitments, *The Snapper*, *The Van* and
Smile, two collections of short stories, and *Rory
& Ita,* a memoir about his parents. He won the
Booker Prize in 19   *ia H*

ALSO BY RODDY DOYLE

Fiction

The Commitments
The Snapper
The Van
Paddy Clarke Ha Ha Ha
The Woman Who Walked Into Doors
A Star Called Henry
Oh, Play That Thing
Paula Spencer
The Deportees
The Dead Republic
Bullfighting
Two Pints
The Guts
Two More Pints
Smile
Two for the Road

Non-Fiction

Rory & Ita
The Second Half (with Roy Keane)

Plays

The Snapper
Brownbread
War
Guess Who's Coming For Dinner
The Woman Who Walked Into Doors
The Government Inspector (translation)
Two Pints

For Children

The Giggler Treatment
Rover Saves Christmas
The Meanwhile Adventures
Wilderness
Her Mother's Face
A Greyhound of a Girl
Brilliant
Rover and the Big Fat Baby

RODDY DOYLE

Charlie Savage

VINTAGE

1 3 5 7 9 10 8 6 4 2

Vintage
20 Vauxhall Bridge Road
London SW1V 2SA

Vintage is part of the Penguin Random House group
of companies whose addresses can be found
at global.penguinrandomhouse.com

First published by Jonathan Cape in 2019
First published in Vintage in 2020

penguin.co.uk/vintage

A CIP catalogue record for this book is available
from the British Library

ISBN 9781784709570

Printed and bound in Great Britain by Clays Ltd, Elcograf S.p.A.

Penguin Random House is committed to a sustainable future for
our business, our readers and our planet. This book is made
from Forest Stewardship Council® certified paper.

For Ronnie Caraher

Acknowledgements

Thanks to Fiona Ness, Ben Hickey, Fionnan Sheahan, John Sutton, and Lucy Luck.

1

One of the grandkids wants a tattoo.

–He's only three, I tell the wife.

–I'm aware of that, she tells me back. –But he still wants one.

–He can't even say 'tattoo', I tell her.

–I know.

–'Hattoo' is what he says.

–I know, she says. –It's sweet.

And she's right. Normally, I don't have much room for the word 'sweet'. If I hear of an adult being described as sweet, I'm off for the hills and I stay up there till they're gone. 'Sweet' is just a different word for 'mad', 'boring', or 'nearly dead', and often it's all three. But kids – little kids – that's different. Especially if they're your own. *Only* if they're your own. No man really cares about other people's kids or grandkids.

Anyway.

–What sort of a present is a tattoo? I ask the wife.

–He has his heart set on one, she says.

Those words terrify me. I once ended up in Wales on Christmas Eve, looking for a Tamagotchi. Dublin was full of the things but the daughter's heart was set

1

on a pink one. And Wales, as everyone knows, is the home of the pink Tamagotchis. They breed there, or something.

Then there was the wife's sister's husband. He wanted us all to walk across the Sahara with him for his fiftieth birthday.

–Will Dollymount not do him? I said. –There's loads of sand and the pint's better.

–He has his heart set on it, said the wife. –And he doesn't drink.

–He'll regret that when he's halfway across the fuckin' Sahara, I said.

–You're gas, she said.

And she booked the tickets, Easyjet to Casablanca. But then, thank Christ, they split up, him and the wife's sister, just before his birthday and he had to go on his own. The last we heard – an Instagram message to one of their kids – he was after joining up with ISIS. But I'm betting they threw him out for being such a pain in the hole.

Anyway. This was different. This was way more complicated than the boat to Holyhead or a plane to Morocco.

–A tattoo, but, I say. –Santy doesn't deliver tattoos, does he?

There's no way I'm letting Santy down the chimney with needles and ink, even if he brings all the sterilisation equipment and a team of elves with verifiable first-aid experience.

–Well, says the wife. –He's after writing the letter.

–He can't write, but, I say. –He's only three.

–He dictated it, she says.

–And it's gone into the postbox?

–Yep.

–Could we not persuade him to change his mind? I ask her. –He could dictate a new letter. 'Dear Santy, on second thoughts, I'd much prefer a scooter.' And what gobshite brought him to the postbox?

She doesn't even stare at me. She just walks out of the kitchen.

–Well, that's helpful, I call after her.

I don't often have good ideas, those light-bulb ones that go off in your head. But now I have two on the trot. And I run after the wife with the first one. This is two days after she walked out – but that's a different story.

–Typhoid Mary, I say.

–What about her?

Mary lives next door. She was there before we moved in. She was probably there before the houses were built.

Anyway.

–You know that tattoo she has between her shoulder blades? I say. –The seagull.

–It's down near her arse, she corrects me.

–Exactly, I say. –But it was up on her shoulders when she got it done thirty years ago.

–So, says the wife.

And I can tell; she's enjoying this.

–You want to traumatise the poor child by bringing Mary in and making him look at her migrating tattoo – and it's not a seagull, by the way, it's a butterfly. You want Mary to get up out of her wheelchair and turn around and—

–Okay, I say. –Forget it.

And I'm turning away, all set to emigrate, when the second idea slaps me.

–I'll do it, I tell her.

–Do what? she says.

–Get the tattoo, I say.

–Go on, she says.

–Well, I explain. –Santy writes back. No problem with the tattoo but you're too young. So we'll put it on your grandad and he can mind it for you and you can look at it any time you want, till you're old enough to have it yourself, on your arm or whatever.

–His chest, she says.

And she's looking at me with – well, it's not admiration, exactly. But it's like she's opened an empty tin of biscuits and discovered there's one left.

So, that's Christmas Eve sorted. I'm heading to a tattoo parlour in town – the daughter says she knows a good one for older people, called Wandering Skin, but I think she might be messing – and I'll be coming home with SpongeBob SquarePants hiding under my shirt.

2

I'm having a slow pint with my buddy.

The grandson has had me plagued all day, wanting to check on his SpongeBob tattoo. My fingers are raw from doing and undoing the buttons of my shirt. What happened was, I'd had to have the hair shaved off my chest when I was getting the tattoo done on Christmas Eve, and the hair has started to grow back. It's grey, like, and it made SpongeBob look like he'd died in the night. The poor kid cried when he saw it and he told his mammy – my daughter – that I'd murdered SpongeBob.

–G'anda 'urder 'PungeBob!

–I didn't touch SpongeBob, I said.

The women looked at me like I was Jimmy Savile, so now I'm having to shave my chest twice a day. I'm standing in front of the mirror, and I've cut myself twice already – poor oul' SpongeBob is bleeding to death. I'm half-thinking of carving him out and just giving him to the child in a plastic bag, when the text arrives.

Pint?

So here we are.

–I've made a new year's resolution, my buddy tells me.

This is unusual. We don't go in for that kind of shite – resolutions and birthdays and that. So something's up. I'm beginning to wish I was back in the bathroom skinning SpongeBob.

–A resolution? I say.

–Yeah, he says. –I've decided. From now on, I'm going to be honest.

I know he's looking at me, but I'm staring at my pint. He's going to say something – I know he is – something embarrassing or sad. He's my friend and all but I'm hoping to Christ he sticks to the football.

But he doesn't.

–I identify as a woman, he says.

And now I look at him. He's sixty or so, same as myself.

–But, I say. –Like – you're a man.

–I know, he says.

–You're dressed the same as always.

–I know.

–You're drinking a pint.

–I know.

–And you're telling me you're a woman?

–I didn't say that, he says. –I said I identify as a woman.

I'm not as shocked as I think I probably should be – and that, in itself, is a bit of a shock. I think my buddy here is after telling me he wishes he was a woman. But I don't seem to care that much. I'm tempted to pat him on the back but I'm worried I'll feel a bra strap under his hoodie.

Anyway.

–What's it mean? I ask him. –Exactly – that you identify as a woman.

We're not shouting, by the way. This is a very quiet conversation.

–I'm not sure, he says. –But I heard it on the radio and I just thought to myself, 'That's me.' It felt right.

–And tell us, I say. –Are you a lesbian?

–What?

–Cos it would probably be handier if you were.

–How would it? he asks.

–When we talk about women.

–We never talk about women.

–*If* we did, I say. –If a good-looking woman walked in now, say. We could both agree on that. It'd be nice.

He shrugs – exactly the same way he's been shrugging for the twenty–five years I've known him. He tells me not to tell anyone and I promise him I won't. But I tell the wife. I'm a bit lost, and in need of a bit of guidance.

–A good buddy of mine says he identifies as a woman, I tell her.

–Which one? the wife asks me.

–He wishes to remain anonymous, I say.

–Is it – ?

And she names him.

–Good Jesus, I say. –How did you know?

–Ah, well, she says, and then the grandson comes in, wanting to assess SpongeBob. So that's that until later, when we're up in the bed.

The wife has a theory. His wife – my pal's wife, like – died a while back, three years or so. Maybe more – I don't trust myself with time any more. Anyway, she says – my wife – that he misses her.

–Yeah, I agree. –That's true.

–And maybe he misses her more than he'd miss himself, she says.

–D'you think?

–It's just a theory, she says.

When she says that – and she says it a good bit, especially since she did that Open University yoke a few years back. But when she says it – *it's just a theory* – you know it isn't *just* anything. It's gospel.

–Fair enough, I say. –That makes sense – sort of. But why's he after telling me?

–Well, you're his friend, she says. –You should be pleased.

And I am. And a bit sad. And – I don't tell her this – a bit excited.

–What about you? she says.

She shifts in the bed and I know there's a big question coming.

–If I go before you, will you identify as a woman?

I keep staring at my book.

–I'd like a sports question, please.

3

I'm heading into town with the daughter. Normally, this would be grand. We'd have a wander and a laugh and maybe a drink on the way home. But this is different. I have to buy clothes. The wife used to come with me but she slapped an embargo on it the last time, about two years ago – maybe three years.

–Never again, she said, when I told her that the shirt she'd said was perfect made me look like Mary Tyler Moore. I'd forgotten all about that. But she hasn't. It was what she called the second-last straw.

Anyway.

I hate clothes.

I could look at a jumper for days and still not know if it's the one for me – or even if it's definitely a jumper. So the daughter has agreed to come with me.

–Grand, so, she says. –I'll be your fashion consultant.

–I'm only buying a pair of jeans and a couple of shirts, I tell her.

–There's no such word as 'only', Dad, she says. – Not in the world of high fashion. Think 'big', think 'statement'.

But I think 'Good', I think 'Jesus', and I think I'll go hide in the attic till she's forgotten all about it.

But I catch her looking at me.

–What?

–I'm looking at your eyes, she says.

–Why?

–We start with the eyes, like, and build from there, she says.

–My eyes don't wear trousers, love, I tell her.

But she's not listening. She's taking a photograph – before I know what she's doing – and she fires it off to her friends.

–Why?

–To find out what colour your eyes are, she says.

–They're brown, I tell her. –I think. At least, they used to be.

Her phone starts pinging and she's reading out her messages.

–Megan says yellow, Sally says puke green and Mark says you must have been a ride before the Famine.

–Mark?

–D'you want his number?

–Ah, here, I say, and I text my pal, the Secret Woman. *Pint?*

So here we are.

–I have to buy new clothes, I tell him.

–Hate that, he says.

–I was hoping you'd come into town with me, I say. –Give me a hand.

–No way, he says. –You're on your own.

I look at him now; I actually stare at him.

–I thought you identified as a woman, I say.

–Yeah, he says. –A woman with enough cop-on never to go shopping for clothes with a colour-blind oul' fella.

–Who says I'm colour-blind?

–Look at your jumper, he says. –Look at your shirt. Clash, clash, clash.

He's hopeless, no good to me. So I'm stuck with the daughter and I'm terrified. Saying no to the wife is easy; it's a big part of the gig. But the daughter – I could never say no to the daughter.

She brings us into the place that used to be Roche's Stores and I think I'm on safe enough ground. But then – Christ – she gets me to put on a pair of trousers and I don't think they're trousers at all.

She shakes the changing-room curtain.

–Are you alright in there?

–I don't think these are meant for a man, love, I say. –I think they're for a big girl. There's no zip.

–It's at the side, like.

–It's no good to me there, love, I tell her. –Can I not just have a pair of Wranglers?

–Try this, she says, and she hands in some sort of a one-sleeved jacket.

I want to cry – I nearly do. She's not going to let me out of the changing room unless I commit to becoming a cartoon. I'm thinking of digging a tunnel when she hands me in something that's almost definitely a shirt. It has a collar and all. I try it on and I show her.

–Blue's your colour, Dad, she says.

–Can we go home now, please? I ask her.

But she's only starting. For the next three hours – I think it's hours but it might be days, or weeks – I stop having opinions and a personality and I just surrender. I only put the foot down when she thinks she's deciding which pub we'll be going to on the way home.

So we're sitting in the Flowing Tide and I'm looking at her over all my shopping bags. I like a pint, I rarely need a pint – but I need the one in front of me now. I'm exhausted, and relieved – a bit hysterical; it must have been like this for the lads coming home from Vietnam. And I admit it, I'm kind of looking forward to getting into the new gear. I smile at her as I pick up my pint, and she says it.

–I'm proud of you, Dad. You're a real metrosexual.

I put the glass down.

–I'm a what?

4

I'm only putting the pint to my lips when the text goes off in my pocket. It's the daughter. The grandson wants to say night-night to SpongeBob. I look at the text, I look at the pint. I'll send her a photo. I'll unbutton the new shirt, do a SpongeBob selfie, and fire it back to her to show the kid before she tucks him in.

One of the sons showed me how to do that – send a photograph on your phone – when he was sending a picture of his dislocated kneecap to his girlfriend in the Philippines – because she's a nurse, he said.

–Is she on her holidays over there? I asked him.

–No.

–Does she live there?

–Yeah.

–Come here, I said. –Have you actually met the girl?

–No, he said. –Not really.

I tried not to sound too taken aback.

–And she's your fuckin' girlfriend?

He muttered something.

–What?

–One of them, he said.

–And do any of your other girlfriends actually live in Dublin? I asked him.

–Think so, he said.

I decided I'd talk to the wife about it – my only wife, by the way – but, not for the first or the last time, I forgot.

Anyway.

I'd be worried she'd tell me she had three more husbands in Cambodia and a toy boy somewhere in Kimmage. Do toy boys still exist, even? I haven't heard mention of one in ages. Maybe they're all retired, or upskilling.

Anyway.

It's my own fault, forgetting to let the grandson say night-night to the tattoo before I left the house. The child is entitled to the real thing, the flesh and blood SpongeBob.

–Mind my pint, I say, and I leg it home.

Legging it isn't what it used to be. Legging it these days means running for three or four steps, then holding my jacket shut and walking as fast as I can without toppling over. But I make it home and up the stairs – just have a short break on the landing. In to the grandson – he waves at SpongeBob. Then I leg it back to the local.

So here we are.

The pint is fine and the Secret Woman is still sitting where I left him. We say nothing for a bit. And I like that, saying nothing. But there's something I've been meaning to ask him.

–What sort of men do you go for?

–I don't, he says.

–You identify as a woman, I remind him.

–Yeah, he says. –But I'm kind of a retired woman.

I want to ask him about the whole internet thing, dating and that. I thought maybe he'd have been

14

surfing for mature men who like men who identify as women, or mature women who identify as men. I never bought a book on the net, never mind a life partner, so I haven't a clue. And I'm worried about the son – a bit.

–I'm not gay, he tells me now. –Just to be clear.

–Grand.

–It's just—, he says, and stops.

He's said nothing about my new shirt or jeans, by the way – the ones the daughter made me buy in town. He might think he's a woman but he's still a bollix.

–It's the gentleness and that, he says. –You know, the things that women have that we don't?

–Yeah, I say.

–That's it, he says. –That's what I want – to be near to, I suppose. The gentleness and the – I don't know. The feminine stuff. Am I making sense?

I don't remember his wife being particularly gentle or anything. She was a nice woman and all but she gave me a dig once – a friendly dig at a party, like – and let's just say I felt it. Let's just say I took a couple of Nurofen when I got home. But I do know what he means. The wife – my wife, like – takes no prisoners but when she puts her hair behind her ear, the way she does that, the little flick, it makes me feel like the luckiest man in the world.

–Yeah, I say. –You're making sense.

–I'm taking steps, he says.

–What?

–To becoming a woman, he says.

–What? I say. –You're taking the tablets – the hormone yokes?

–No.

–Not the whole shebang? The operation?

15

– Calm down, for Jaysis sake, he says. –No, I'm after joining a book club.

–That's your first step to womanhood?

–It's a start, he says.

He's right, I suppose. I never met a man who was in one. I asked the wife once what her book club involved and she told me to mind my own business; it was a secret world, she said, that not even the Russians could penetrate.

Anyway.

I'm happy for him – I think.

–You didn't notice my shirt, I say.

–Is that you? he says. –For a minute there I thought I was sitting beside Jamie Redknapp.

5

The wife wants to go to a spa.

I asked her what she wanted for her birthday and that's what she came up with. It serves me right. Why didn't I just get her a scarf or one of those One4all vouchers – or even both?

The problem is, she expects me to go with her. I went to a Christian Brothers school and it wasn't a happy time; they were mad bastards there. But I'd rather go back to the Brothers for a year than go to a spa for a long weekend. You knew where you were with the Christian Brothers. But I'm not even sure what a spa is.

I'm looking at one on the laptop when the daughter walks into the kitchen.

–What's that? she asks.

–A spa, I tell her.

It's actually a photo of about ten women in white dressing gowns, and a man – he's in a dressing gown too. The women look like they're having a great time but the man looks a bit lost. Not lost, exactly – his face reminds me of Fredo's in *The Godfather* when he knows he's going to be shot.

–It looks fab, says the daughter.

–Does it?

–Ah, yeah, she says.

I point at the man.

–Look at that poor sap.

–What's wrong with him? she says. –That's just a projection, Dad. He probably thinks it's epic. Oh, wow – massage therapy, body treatments, hot stone massage.

I whimper. At least, I think I do. Some sort of noise comes out of me.

–What's wrong with you? she asks me.

–Would I have to do all that? I ask her back. –If I went.

She sits beside me. Actually, she shoves me off the chair and I'm standing beside her as she takes over the laptop.

–There's loads of stuff for men as well, like, she says.

–Is there?

My eyes are swimming, she's hopping from page to page so fast.

–Look, she says. –Cool. There's a man package.

–A what?

–Deep tissue massage, hammam, and Indian head massage. Will I book one for you?

I whimper again.

–Poor Dad, she says. –The first two days are the worst, like.

I point at the screen.

–Would I at least be able to watch *Soccer Saturday* while they're doing the Indian thing to my head?

–Mammy will love it, she says.

She's right, and that's the main thing. I try really hard to believe that.

–Perfect, says the daughter.

–What?

18

–There's a couples pamper package.

–Ah, Jesus.

I go out the back for some air. There's a rope in the shed and I might hang myself while I'm out there. The dogs think I'm bringing them for a walk but then they see that I'm shaking and they sit – all of them – and stare at me.

–No walkies today, lads, I tell them. –Daddy's having a coconut rub.

The thing is, there's something up with the wife. It's not anything midlife – we left that behind years ago. It's nothing bad or too dramatic but there's definitely something up.

–How many menopauses does the average woman have? I ask my pal, the Secret Woman.

–Give us a chance, he says. –I'm only after getting here.

–We've been here for hours, I tell him.

We're in the local, looking at the third pints settling.

–I mean becoming a woman, he says. –It's all new to me.

–The shift from male to female, I say. –Maybe that's *your* menopause.

He stares at me.

–Maybe you could take that idea and shove it up *your* hole, he says.

–I rest my case, I say back.

But back to the wife. She's restless, constantly wanting to do stuff. She's always been like that and it's one of the things I've always – well – loved about her. But this is different, somehow. She's on the go all the time.

–It'll force her to relax, says the daughter.

And she's right – again.

–Book it there for us, love, I say. –Where is it, by the way?

–Roscommon.

–Ah Jesus, is there nowhere a bit nearer?

But that's us, me and the wife – we're heading to Roscommon for the wife's birthday. I'm driving and she has the spa website up on her phone. She's booking the treatments she wants. She's excited – I can tell. And it's nice.

–What sort of a wrap do you want? she asks me.

–A wrap? I say.

Things are looking up.

–Tandoori chicken.

–It's not on the list, she says. –You can have a muscle-ease ocean wrap, an exotic frangipani body nourish wrap or a dry flotation.

We're going past Mullingar, so there's no turning back.

–Fuck it, I say. –Put me down for the dry flotation.

It sounds harmless enough.

–Does it come with chips? I ask her.

–I doubt it, she says. –Unless you're floating in vinegar.

6

I've found out what spas are really about: cakes.

And gin.

I'm stuck in a spa in Roscommon for the wife's fifty-ninth. There's candles all over the place, on the floor and all. I'm tripping over the things everywhere I go. I nearly set fire to myself. Actually, I *do* set fire to myself. I don't know how I do it, but I manage to drag the cord of my dressing gown right across the flame of one of the bloody candles and, before I even know I'm close to death, a beautician and a masseuse are charging at me with matching fire extinguishers. I'm only in the place half an hour!

My eyebrows are singed and the young one – the beautician – offers to fix them, half-price. I think she's afraid I'm going to sue them for nearly cremating me. But she isn't looking at my eyebrows when the offer comes in. She's staring at SpongeBob on my chest. What's left of the dressing gown is on the black tiles, beside the line of candles. I'm standing there in my boxers and socks, and I'm wondering if I should maybe have taken the socks off before I left the room, and I'm thinking I probably should have. I'm feeling far from home; I've woken up in *Mean Girls* or something.

–Nice tatt, she says.

I'm guessing that 'tatt' is short for 'tattoo'.

–It's not really mine, I tell her, and I explain that it belongs to the grandson and I'm only minding it for him. And, suddenly, I'm not in *Mean Girls* any more; I'm in *Bambi*, surrounded by little woodland creatures and a few fairly big ones, all of them smelling of nail polish and marzipan. It's the sweetest thing they've ever heard. I'm Celebrity Grandad and they all want selfies with SpongeBob.

I'm mortified but, really, it's not too bad. Tara the beautician follows West Ham and the lad who does my nails has a cousin who knows Conor McGregor. It's a pleasant way to kill an hour and I come away with a voucher for €50 and a brand new pair of eyebrows.

I'm back in the room before I think about the wife. Where was she during my remake of *Towering Inferno*? I'm thinking about sending the Secret Woman a picture of my eyebrows – *Feast your eyes lol* – when a text comes in from the wife. *In the thermal suite x*.

It's the *x* that does it. It's her birthday, the reason we're here. So I'm back slaloming through the candles, and I find her sitting in some kind of a big egg, looking out at a couple of trees and a field. It's hot – it's very hot. She's been reading her book but it's become a bit warped and some of the pages have fallen out.

–It's lovely here, she says.

–Yeah.

–Really lovely, she says.

–Yeah.

–So tranquil, she says.

–Yeah.

–Time for a drink, she says.

–Now we're fuckin' talking.

She smiles at me – and stops.

–What happened to your eyebrows?

–They're new, I tell her. –I'm thinking of getting a power booster facial as well. They said it'll take five years off me – at least. I'll fill you in when we get to the bar.

And that's when we discover the cakes.

The place is full of women eating cakes. They're all in their dressing gowns, some with their faces covered in mud, and they're sitting at round tables – there must be forty tables. And they're scoffing cakes off those tiered cake stands that you used to see in Bewley's years ago. Some of them are laughing and chatting. But most of them are just keeping an eye on one another, making sure no one gets a bun she's not entitled to.

You can tell – it's in the body language and the eyes: they're here for the cakes. That's the real purpose of the dressing gowns; the crumbs and the goo can go everywhere.

–Do you want a tray of cakes? I ask the wife.

–I don't, she says. –I'm having a gin.

–Grand, I say.

–A Hendricks and Fever Tree.

I leg it to the bar before I forget the name. I give the barman €20 and I wait for the change. He stands there and waits for more money. I give in first.

There's a slice of cucumber in her glass.

–He put vegetables in your gin, I tell her.

I'm worried now that he sneaked diced carrots into my pint. It might be what they do to the drink in spas.

A fight's after breaking out at one of the tables. There's a woman skulling her mother – she looks like her mother – with a cake stand. There's blood on the dressing gowns.

The wife picks up her glass.

–A journey to tranquillity, harmony and balance, she says. –Cheers.

And – head right back – she laughs.

7

I've no idea where I am; I haven't a clue. I'm not at home. The room's all wrong, I'm on the wrong side of the bed.

I'm staring at a candle.

–We're still in the spa.

–We are.

–Did you hit me?

–No, she says.

It's the wife, by the way.

–I nudged you, she says.

–Nudged?

–Yeah.

–Cassius Clay nudged Sonny Liston, I say.

–I tapped you with one of my toes, she says. –Because, first, you were snoring and, second, you've gone viral.

–I've gone what?

I sit up in the bed – I try to sit up. It usen't to be a problem; sitting up came naturally. Now I need a crane and planning permission. Things creak, things wobble, things teeter and threaten to collapse. But I make it.

–Don't pretend you don't know what going viral means, she says.

–But I don't know what it means.

–I know you, she says. –You're going to pretend you think going viral means catching the bird flu or AIDS or something.

She's spot on.

–That's rubbish, I say.

I have to deny it. It's either that or admit I'm hopelessly predictable and a bit of a gobshite.

–Look it, she says.

She's holding her phone the way Wyatt Earp used to hold his gun. And it's aimed at me.

I'd better be clear here: she isn't being aggressive – at all. She's just kicked me awake but she's smiling; she's enjoying herself, having the crack.

The screen of her phone is swimming in front of me.

–Hang on, I say. –I need my reading glasses.

I've three pairs of glasses – my ordinary ones, my reading ones, and a pair for driving. I once drove all the way to Wexford wearing my reading glasses. I'd picked up the wrong ones on the way out of the house and I was going through Kilmacanogue before I realised that the only thing I could see clearly was the dashboard.

Anyway.

The specs are on the floor beside the bed. I get them on and see what's gone viral. My chest, nipples and all – and SpongeBob. And a young lad, right under my armpit, pointing at SpongeBob and grinning.

–That's Brendan, I say.

–Who's Brendan?

–He did my nails yesterday, I tell her. –Nice enough chap. He trimmed the hair in my ears as well.

–Look, she says.

She's pointing at the number under the pic. *207K*.

–Is that Facebook? I ask.

–It is.

–And two hundred and seven thousand people have 'liked' the picture?

–So far.

–And that's what 'going viral' is, is it?

–I think so, she says.

–At least it's just my chest, I say. –My face isn't in the picture.

She flicks her finger across the screen and there I am, all of me this time, with Tara the beautician under my other armpit.

–Oh.

–'Oh' is right, she says. –You don't want to read the comments.

And she reads them to me.

–'Gross', 'barf', 'blech', 'yucky', 'sick', 'who's the paedo?', 'who's the leper?', 'is that Donald Trump or SpongeBob between his boobs?', 'nice legs, shame about the face'.

She looks up from the phone.

–I could go on, she says.

–It might be better if you don't, I say. –Did no one say anything nice?

–There was one, she says. –Somewhere – hang on.

She reads.

–'When did you get the job in the undertakers, Tara?'

–Is that the only positive one? I ask.

–There's a few more, she says. –'Sweet', 'ah, bless', 'you've done worse, Bren'.

She climbs out of the bed and grabs her dressing gown.

–Are we heading down to the thermal suite? I ask her.

–No, she says. –We're rocking up to the bar.

–It's still dark out, I say.

–We can watch the dawn together, she says.

Do they have dawns in Roscommon?

–Come on, Groucho, she says, and she heads for the door.

Why did she call me Groucho? I'm going to check my new eyebrows with the reading glasses on. But then I remember: the last time I looked at myself when I was wearing reading glasses, I confronted my own mortality – and all I'd wanted to do was brush my teeth. So I throw the glasses on the bed and follow the wife.

I find her outside on the patio, with a bowl of muesli and a gin and tonic.

I sit beside her.

–D'you not like it here? I ask.

–Love it, she says. –But—.

She puts down her spoon and picks up her glass.

–The whole harmony and tranquillity thing, she says. –It's not for me.

She looks at me.

–I want to go viral as well, she says. –I want to do something.

–Not a tattoo.

–No, she says. –Not necessarily. And I don't mean literally going viral. But something a bit mad. Old age can fuck off. Am I right?

–Bang on.

8

I'm a bit worried about one of the sons. I'm not sure why. Maybe because his girlfriend is a woman he's never actually met. She might not be a girl at all, for all I know. She might be a man – or a gang of men – hiding behind a photograph.

Don't get me wrong – I'm not too worried about any of my children, the daughter or any of the sons. They're all grand. And this lad, the one with the phantom mott in the Philippines, he's perfectly alright. He has a job and he shares a house with a bunch of lads. I was in it once and was surprised not to find Mother Teresa in there with them, because the place was an absolute kip. It made the Black Hole of Calcutta look like the Japanese Gardens. But at the same time I found it reassuring, the dirt, the bins, the cans, the techno – I think that's the word for the shite they were listening to. And there he was, in all that normality – normality defined by a houseful of young lads. I came away happy.

I doubt if Mother Teresa had much time for techno. Duran Duran would have been more her thing – or was that Lady Di?

Anyway.

I don't understand the whole internet dating thing. When I met the wife I asked her if she wanted to dance. She said 'I suppose so', and we were married a year later. No need for Tinder or Elite Dating or any of the internet stuff. She got sick on my shoes that night and I think that's why she agreed to marry me – but that's a different story.

Anyway, I speak to one of the other sons about it. He's going out with a girl he met on the internet as well.

–You actually get to meet her now and again, but, do you? I ask him.

–Da, he says. –We're married.

–Was that you?

–Yeah.

–Grand, I say. –And everything's good, yeah?

–Sound, yeah, he says. –That baby on your lap there.

–She's yours?

–Yeah.

How come I can remember the name of Lady Di's favourite band but I can't remember which of my children is married? That's happening a lot these days. I know that the Lone Ranger's horse was called Silver but I don't know what colour my car is – unless I go out and look at it – never mind the parents of the baby perched on my knee.

She's a dote, by the way – the new granddaughter. The house is full of grandkids today; they're charging up and down the stairs, thumping all around the place. The dogs are refusing to come in from the garden.

–So, I say to the son. –You met—

–Jess.

–You met Jess on the internet and then you arranged to meet – in the flesh, like.

–Yeah.

–Grand.

–You must have looked up someone on Facebook, he says. –Some old flame.

–No, I lie. –Never.

–Well, if you did, he says. –People do it all the time. Meeting new people, tracking down old girlfriends. It's the way it is, like.

I did actually search for an old girlfriend once, on Facebook, when the wife was out at her book club. The problem was, I couldn't remember her surname. So I typed in her first name – Eileen. There were millions of them, of course, all over the world, not just Ireland – including one who called herself *Come on Eileen*. I gave up on Eileen and typed in the name of a girl I'd gone with for three days when I was twelve. I could remember both of her names, which felt like a bit of a triumph. And I found her. She described herself as a recovering chocoholic and a graduate of the School of Hard Knocks; there was a picture of a cat in the top corner, instead of her face.

–So, anyway, I say to the son in the kitchen. –Your brother's after connecting with a girl he's never going to meet. She's over in the Philippines – the other side of the world. Is he hiding something? Is he gay – is that it?

The daughter walks in just when I say that.

–There's nothing wrong with being gay, Dad, she says.

–I know that, I say. –I never said there was.

–Lots of footballers are gay.

–Yeah, I say. –They play for West Ham.

–You can't say that, Dad.

–Ah, I know, I say.

But I don't know.

How do you tell a boy who you think might be gay, but mightn't be, that you don't mind what he is, gay, straight or whatever – that you just love him – when you can't even say the word 'gay' without feeling guilty or stupid, or old, or angry – or wrong?

The granddaughter's fallen asleep.

I kiss the top of her head.

9

–What did you do to your eyebrows? my pal, the Secret Woman, asks me.

–Nothing, I say.

They're nearly back to normal, the eyebrows. But they still make me look a bit like Grace Jones after a decade-long binge.

–A bit of fire damage, I say. –That's all. How was the book club?

–Well, he says. –Grand.

The word 'grand' can carry many meanings – 'great', 'okay', 'brilliant', 'not too bad', 'not that great', 'fairly shite', 'I don't understand', 'we'll see how it goes', and sometimes, just now and again, it means 'grand'. The Secret Woman's 'grand' here means 'grand, but'. He's joined the book club as a first, experimental step to full-blown womanhood. But it's clear: the poor chap is disappointed.

–They were being a bit cagey, he says.

–The other women?

–Yeah, he says. –With me being there, you know.

–And did you tell them that you identify as a woman? I ask him.

–No, he says. –I was going to, but—.

–What did you wear? I ask him.

We're in the local, same as always. It's packed, which, in a way, is as good as empty. We can say what we like and no one will hear us.

–Well, he says. –You know that shirt I have with the horses on it?

–Yeah – go on.

–I saw this picture of Princess Grace, he explains. –And she was wearing a headscarf with horses on it.

–Did you have the shirt on your head? I ask.

–No, he says.

–It might have been lost on them, so, I say. –The fact that your shirt was a tribute to Princess Grace. What did yis talk about?

–Well, he says. –That's kind of private.

–Oh, you're becoming a woman, alright, I tell him. –Don't worry. Can I ask you just one thing, but?

–Okay, he says. –One question.

–Did yis talk about the book?

–No.

–Thanks, I say. –I always wondered. The wife's leaving her book club, by the way.

It's true. She announced it on our way home from the spa in Roscommon.

–Why? I asked her.

She loves reading; she always has a couple of books on the go.

–Ah, she said.

And she left it at that for a few minutes. The radio was on and I think it was Ryan Tubridy that tipped her over the edge.

–It's boring, she said. –It's too bloody respectable.

–The book club?

–Yeah.

34

–Come here, I said. –You're always in bits the morning after your book club. It can't be that respectable.

–I'll tell you what it is, she said. –I'm *expected* to be in a book club.

She pointed at the car radio.

–*He* expects me to be in a book club. They all expect me to be in a book club. Because I'm a middle-aged woman. Even if we never read the books.

–Do yis not read the books?

–Mind your own business, she said. –And anyway, I won't have time for the book club any more.

–How come? I asked.

–Carmel wants me to be her roadie.

Carmel is the wife's older sister. She's in a band called the Pelvic Floors. If you want to hear punk rock played by a gang of women in their late fifties and early sixties – and I do – then I heartily recommend them.

–That's great, I said.

And I think I meant it; I'm not sure.

–And you know Penny? said the wife. –The drummer?

–Yeah.

–Carmel says if she dies I can take over on the drums, she says.

–Is Penny dying?

–Well, she smokes forty a day and she fainted in the middle of *Alternative Ulster*. She fell right over the drums.

–Oh, well, I said. –Fingers crossed, so.

We get home and I tell the daughter that her mammy's about to become a rock chick. There must have been something in my voice, because—

–What's wrong with that, like? says the daughter.

35

–Nothing, I say back. –Nothing at all. But she'll be lugging amps and speakers and that.

–Yeah, says the daughter. –So?

–With her back?

–With what back? says the daughter. –There's nothing wrong with Mammy's back.

She's right. It's just an automatic thing. Nearly everyone I know who's my age has a bad back or a bad hip, or a knee. Until they get a new hip or knee.

Anyway.

–You feel threatened, Dad, says the daughter.

I'm going to deny it, but I don't. She's probably right – again – and I've always loved watching her being right, even when it means that I've been wrong.

But why don't I want the wife to be in a rock band?

–Think about it, says the daughter. –Who would you prefer to be married to? Peig Sayers or Lady Gaga?

–Good point, love.

–You haven't answered the question, like.

–Well then, I say. –The best of both worlds. Peggy Gaga.

10

I'm watching the Irish version of *Strictly* when I remember Eileen's surname.

I used to go with this girl called Eileen when I was about sixteen. Actually, I was sixteen years, four months, and seven days old when she let me put my hand on some of the secrets under her jumper. Anyway, I tried to find her on Facebook – for no particular reason, really, just to see how it all worked. But I couldn't remember what came after 'Eileen'. I could remember the name of her dog, I could remember that she'd loved Alvin Stardust, but I couldn't remember her bloody surname.

So, we're watching poor Des Cahill when the name pops into my head.

–Pidgeon!

–He's not that bad, in fairness, says the wife.

–Ah, he is, I say.

I'm a man who shouts at the telly. Football, politics, the reality programmes – I shout at them all. And I'm training the grandkids to do the same. It's a skill I want to pass on so that in years to come they'll look up from their phones now and again and roar at something else.

My three-year-old grandson, the daughter's little lad, is already a master of the art. He shouts 'Gobshite!'

every time he sees Enda Kenny on the News – except he can't pronounce 'gobshite'.

'Hobs'ite!' he squeals.

I even brought him down to the local to show him off. And he didn't let me down.

'Hobs'ite!'

The lads in the pub thought it was class, even the twit in the corner who supports Fine Gael. Then Trump's head appeared on the big screen.

'Uckin' heejit!'

The roof came off the shop.

Anyway, me shouting 'pigeon' at Des Cahill didn't particularly surprise the wife. She enjoys a good shout, herself. Although she prefers to shout at the radio – and the dogs.

Seriously, though, I've no interest in tracking down Eileen Pidgeon, or whatever she's called these days. That young one broke my heart when I found her behind the coal shed with my brother – and it wasn't even one of my big brothers!

Anyway.

Now and again, an old name comes into my head – a lad I'd knocked around with, say, and if I'm near the laptop and I can be bothered, I'll look him up on Facebook. I've found some of the old friends and a good few of them look even worse than I do, which is brilliant. But I've never got in touch with any of them, male or female. I don't want to – or, I don't want to enough.

But it's the thing these days, meeting people online. One of my sons married a girl he met on the internet. I get that – I can understand it. But it's another of the sons that worries me. He says he's going with a girl he's never met. She's a nurse in the Philippines.

–Is she thinking of coming over? I ask him.

–No, he says. –Don't think so.

There's no regret in his voice – no impatience. She's a lovely looking girl. A bit too lovely, even. I'm wondering if she's even real. And I'm wondering if he's maybe hiding himself behind her picture.

–Is he gay? I ask the daughter.

–Ask him yourself, like, she says. –You're his dad.

She's right – it's my job.

So, here we are, me and the son, in the kitchen he shares with a bunch of other lads. The state of the place – I've just turned down a cup of tea because the mug looks like it was robbed from a grave. The kettle seems to have a head of hair.

Anyway.

–Yis have the place looking nice and cosy, I tell him.

–Yeah, he says.

It's freezing. My hands are blue. I feel like I'm already in deep water, so I take the plunge.

Here goes:

–Are you gay, son?

–No, he says.

I've done my homework. I was up googling till two in the morning.

–Are you bisexual, son? I ask him.

–No, he says. –D'you want a biscuit?

–Do you have any?

–Not sure – don't think so.

–Are you intersexual?

–No.

–Pansexual?

–No.

–You know what it means?

–Think so, yeah.

–Grand, I say. –What about polysexual?

He shakes his head.

I'm running out of sexuals. I've a list in my back pocket but I don't want to take it out, like I'm in SuperValu or something.

–Right, son, I say. –I surrender. What are you?

–The one you left out, he says.

–What one's that?

–Heterosexual.

–Are you?

–Yeah.

I'm a bit disappointed after all that. I had my words ready and all, so I say them anyway.

–Well, whatever your orientation, son, I love you.

I'm shaking a bit.

He looks at me, and smiles.

–You're a mad fucker, Da, he says. –I love you too.

–Thanks, son.

11

Years back – this would have been when the daughter had just started school. There was a Christmas show before the holidays, I managed to get a few hours off, and myself and the wife went up to the school. So we're there, and there's a little lad wearing a sheet at the front of the room, and he's holding a plastic hammer and a bit of balsa wood.

–That'll be Joseph, I whisper to the wife. –The carpenter.

–Thanks for that, Charlie, says the wife. –I thought he was an estate agent.

Then the daughter walks in. She's got a blue tea towel on her head and she's carrying a baldy-headed doll under her arm. And she marches right over to Joseph.

–Look, Joseph, she says. –We're after having a baby boy.

That was years ago – the daughter has a real little lad of her own now. But it might as well have happened earlier today because I still feel so proud when I think about it. The way she delivered that line – I believed every word.

I could happily spend the rest of my life just thinking about the moments when my kids and grandkids have made me feel proud. There was the time one of the sons scored the winner – a header, by the way – in the Under-10s summer league's final. It was kind of accidental and his nose hasn't been quite the same since – but it was still a cracking goal.

There was the time the eldest granddaughter phoned Joe Duffy and told him to calm down. She was only seven and it was her granny – the wife – who put her up to it. But it was still her voice on the radio telling Joe to take a Valium.

There was the time another of the sons brought home a dead seagull and tried to nurse it back to life. He was shoving a slice of Brennans bread into its beak when I walked into the kitchen.

–He's hungry, he told me.

–He's a bit more than hungry, son, I told him.

I picked him up and put him on my lap, and he cried and cried and cried – and I never felt happier.

He gulped – and looked up at me.

–Can we give him a proper Christian burial, Da? he said.

–I've a shoebox upstairs waiting for him, I told him. –Blessed by the Pope.

I could go on, because the fact is: everything my kids and their kids have done – everything: the way they learnt to walk and to speak, the way they inhale and exhale, everything – well, nearly everything – has made me happier than I could ever have thought possible. Not just happy, or proud – I feel like an animal and I know I'd do anything to protect them. I'd bite, I'd maim and kill – I'd even miss *Match of the Day* for my kids and grandkids. I think of them and I know I have a heart, because I can feel it pumping, keeping me alive for them.

Then there's the wife.

42

I'm in a pub called The Mercantile on Dame Street, and I'm watching the woman I married nearly forty years ago beating the lard out of a set of drums. She's on the little stage with three other women and I've never seen – or heard – anything like it in my life.

Let me remind you: the wife's sister, Carmel, formed a band called the Pelvic Floors – they play punk and they're all women who are hitting sixty – and she asked the wife to be their roadie. Anyway, the original drummer, Penny, left soon after, due to artistic differences. She wanted to come out from behind the drums and sing a few slowies –*Take My Breath Away* and *Total Eclipse of the Heart* were mentioned. Carmel kicked her out of the band and the wife got in behind the drums before poor Penny had her coat buttoned.

Anyway, it's an Over-fifties Battle of the Bands night and the Pelvic Floors are battering the opposition, three sad bastards who seem to think they're a-ha – one of them even dislocated his shoulder when he threw himself at the wall during the chorus of *Take On Me* – and two lads with guitars who call themselves Fifty Shades of Bald.

Anyway, Carmel is screaming out the words of *White Riot* but my eyes are on the wife – on her hands holding the drumsticks, and on her face.

I'm on my own. And I'm glad I am – because I'm speechless. I wasn't talking to anyone but I know I wouldn't be able to talk back.

Her face! She's not smiling – punks don't smile. But I know: she's happy.

And beautiful.

I feel it before I know it: I'm happy too. I'm bouncing up and down, I'm pogoing – and I never did that when I was twenty.

12

I'm up in Beaumont Hospital visiting the last of the uncles. He's on the way out, slipping in and out of consciousness – mostly out.

It's amazing, really. I don't think he knows who I am any more and I don't think he can really see. But I just asked him to name the England team that won the World Cup in 1966, and he almost sat up.

–In goal, Gordon Banks.

–Just the surnames, Terry, I say. –Don't tire yourself.

–Right back, George Cohen, says Uncle Terry. –Centre backs, Bobby Moore and Big Jack Charlton. Left back – left back—.

His eyes close.

Terry is my mother's little brother. He was only thirteen, I think, when I was born. He'd bring me to the football – Tolka Park, Dalymount. He had a Honda 50, and he got me a helmet of my own. Every Sunday afternoon, straight after the dinner, I'd be standing, waiting at the front door for Uncle Terry. He never let me down.

His eyes open.

–Left back—.

–We'll get back to him, Terry, I say. –What about midfield?

– Alan Ball, he says. –Nobby Styles and the other Charlton, Bobby. Then Martin Peters. But the left back—.

His eyes close.

Men like Terry, men like me – we'll forget our own names and we'll forget that the things at the end of our legs are called feet, but we'll always remember the 1966 World Cup team and who scored for Ireland in Stuttgart – all the other important names and results. The football will cling to the insides of our heads long after everything else has slid out.

Terry's eyes open.

–Just the forwards left, Terry, I remind him.

–Left back—.

–We'll get back to him, I say. –Give us the forwards.

–Centre forwards, says Uncle Terry. –Roger Hunt and—.

His eyes close.

And open.

–Geoff Hurst.

There was a point about fifteen years ago when most of the actors and actresses became 'your man' or 'the young one that used to be in that thing'. I'd forgotten most of the names – the actors and the films.

It's not like that with football. There are young lads playing today who are younger than my oldest grand-kids – if that makes sense – and I've no problem remembering their names. Those two kids that are playing for Everton, Tom Davies and Ademola Look-man – if they were actors in *Peaky Blinders* I wouldn't have a clue who they were, and I'd forget that the thing was called *Peaky Blinders* until the next time I was watching it.

The last time Terry was in the house we watched a match together. (I could tell you the teams, the score, the scorers and the consequences, but I won't.) Anyway, Terry put on what he called his football glasses and he sat up and leaned forward.

–I'm never old when I'm watching the football, Charlie, he said. –I'm the same as I was when I was ten or eleven, there's no difference.

We watched for a while.

–I'm not old, he said. –And the players aren't young. Not when they're playing.

He pointed at the screen.

–Look now, he said. –Eden Hazard's getting ready to come on.

Okay, it was Chelsea v. Spurs.

–Standing there, said Terry. –Waiting to go on – he's a young lad, look. Now he's on – he's run onto the pitch. And look – he's a man. He doesn't have an age.

It was a great game. Four goals, two fights, and Leicester, who weren't even playing, ended up winning the Premiership.

–I'd have been dead years ago if it wasn't for the football, said Terry.

I knew what he meant. At the final whistle I got up to make the tea and I couldn't straighten my legs; I nearly fell over Terry, headfirst into the telly. I'd just played a full ninety minutes of Premiership football and I hadn't even sweated but the trip in to the kettle nearly killed me.

I'm sitting beside Terry now. It's just me and him. Terry never got married – he had no kids.

He opens his eyes.

–Left back –, he says. –Left back—.

But he's gone again – eyes closed.

Terry didn't like the changes in the game, the TV coverage.

–It's become a bloody fashion show, he said once, when we were watching the pundits on Sky at half–time. –With their gel there, and the hankies in their jacket pockets.

It annoyed him; he even threw a biscuit at Thierry Henry, and the dogs went mental, right through the ads and the first ten minutes of the second half.

–That's the future of football, Charlie, he shouted over the dogs. –Thierry Henry's fuckin' cardigan.

Now he opens his eyes.

–Left back, he says.

–Go on, Terry, I say. –Last name – go on.

–Wilson, he says. –Ray Wilson.

13

I've been groaning for years. But for some reason this time they notice. Or, the grandson notices.

–G'anda wusty, he says.

I make 'a deep, inarticulate sound conveying pain, despair, pleasure, etc' (*Oxford English Dictionary*) when I'm standing up after my dinner, and the little lad says I'm rusty.

–We can't have that, says the daughter.

And I know I'm in trouble. Ageing men are supposed to groan; as far as I know it's in the job description. But my groaning days are probably over. The daughter is going to cure me or kill me.

But I'm not going without a protest.

–It was the shepherd's pie, I say.

–What was wrong with it? says the wife, even though it was me who made it.

–Nothing, I say. –The opposite. It was an expression of my professional satisfaction.

That's not altogether true. Straightening the back and the legs at the same time – and at speed – has become a major, and a perilous, operation. I seem to lose contact with the world and the groan is the thing that brings me back down. But I can't tell them that. It's a man's health thing – and men don't have health.

Anyway.

My protests are pointless. I've become the daughter's project – again.

–We'll turn fat into fit, Dad, she says.

–What?

–Better sore than sorry, like.

Just to be clear: I'm not Fatty Arbuckle or Jabba the Hutt. I'm more like O'Connell Street – not great, a bit grim, but grand for the time being. But when the daughter starts talking in slogans she's like Genghis Khan rampaging across central Asia – there's no stopping her.

First it's the gear.

I don't mind the tracksuits too much but she tries to get me into some of the stuff you'd see on Usain Bolt. He seems like a nice lad and all, but I was groaning long before little Usain could even walk; I'm way ahead of him. But she has me in a pair of Usain's shorts and I feel like I'm in underpants that were built for a six-year-old.

–I can't go out in these.

–Not to the pub, like, she reassures me.

–Not anywhere, I say. –I'd be arrested. Or I should be.

She's not listening.

–The performance material is minimalist in design, she explains. –So there's no weighing you down, like, when you're building up a sweat.

–I'm only going for a walk!

–Sweat is fat crying, Dad.

–What fat?

The grandson – the daughter's little lad – is staring at one of my shins. He points.

–Hattoo?

–No, love, I say. –Varicose vein.

The groaning – I prefer 'groaning' to 'grunting'; it has a bit more dignity to it. Anyway, it started years ago. I don't think it's a health issue, or even a part of growing old. I think it's kind of an unconscious protest: 'I don't want to do this.' We groan as we pick up the toys and the shopping, as we get up to answer the door or to find out why there's a child crying in the room next door. We do these things because we have to, and we should – but the groan is the protest, the fight: 'Fuck off and leave me alone.' The groans keep us sane.

It's just a theory.

And it's clearly bolloxology, because I've been groaning nonstop but I'm still rigged out like Oscar Pistorius – and I'm only bringing the dogs for a walk around the block.

And now she's taking a photograph of me!

–What're you doing?

–Don't worry, she says. –It's just for the WhatsApp group.

–What WhatsApp group? I say.

–The family group, she says.

Suddenly, she looks caught, guilty. I haven't seen that look since I caught her taking two euro out of the Trócaire box, years ago.

–What family? I ask her.

–Ours.

We both seem to be speechless – for a bit. I decide not to tell her that I don't know what WhatsApp is. The explanation would get in the way.

I have to speak – it's up to me. I make sure I don't groan.

–How come I'm not in the group? I ask.

–It's – like. We're worried about you.

–Why?

She doesn't answer. She's crying now, though – and I suppose that's the answer.

–I'm just getting old, love, I tell her.

–Yeah, she says. –But it's crap, like.

–That's true, I say. –But look it.

The grandson is hugging my Spandex-covered leg.

–If I wasn't getting old I wouldn't be this fella's grandad, I tell her. –And have you any idea how happy being his grandad makes me feel?

She nods – she smiles.

–It's just part of the package, love, I say.

I shrug. She nods – she understands.

–Can I get back into my trousers? I ask.

–Okay, she says. –Then we can discuss your diet, like.

I groan – I actually grunt.

14

–Sardines fight cancer, Dad, says the daughter.

–No, they don't, love, I tell her – The average sardine couldn't give a shite about cancer. Or anything else for that matter.

–You're gas, she says, sounding very like her mother.

I'm looking down at a tin of the things – sardines – on the kitchen table. They disgust me, even with the lid still covering them. I know they're in there, in a row, like an execution squad. The evil, oily bastards – I hate them. And I know I'm going to eat them.

I've been arguing with the daughter for days now. She's determined to change my lifestyle, just because I groan occasionally – when I stand up, say, or sit down or open the fridge or turn the page of the paper or press a button on the remote, or most activities, really – even thinking. I tried to explain it to her, that it's just getting older and the groaning comes with the wrinkles, the ear hair and the – eh – the forgetfulness. And, in fairness, she calmed down on the exercise. I was able to persuade her that I'm never going to represent Ireland on the parallel bars and that a walk most days is as much as I need to keep the heart in order.

But she came back hard with the diet. She has me eating things that I never knew existed. She's been making me swallow stuff that might not even be food – or is rotten. 'Fermented' is the word she's using but I might as well be eating the sludge at the bottom of the brown wheelie. Sauerkraut might do great things to the digestive tract – whatever that is exactly – but I've been farting away like the Orient Express on that long stretch between Bucharest and Constantinople. I even had to go out and stand in the garden last night – the poor dogs tried to excape over the back wall. The sauerkraut is turning me into a very lonely man. But I'll keep eating it.

Because of the grandson.

Every time I raise an objection he steps out from behind the daughter and he stares up at me with those big eyes that are so exactly like hers.

–Okay, okay, I say, and I immediately pull the lid off the sardines, put my head back like a cormorant and swallow them. I shovel the sauerkraut into me and stand out in the garden in the hail and sleet while the dogs howl and bite their own tails.

Power food, me hole.

–You are what you eat, Dad, she says.

–I'm not a fuckin' fish, I'd tell her if there wasn't a sardine trying to fight its way back up my throat.

Love is killing me.

I don't think I'm a fussy eater. I have no objection to vegetables as long as I've seen them before and I know what they're called. I'm not fussed about the colour; they don't have to be green. I'll eat them even if I don't particularly like them. All I ask, really, is that they look like they grew out of the ground, and on this planet.

But she's going into some health food shop in town – The Joys of Gravel, or something – and she's bringing home little packets of roots and peelings that, under a certain light, look extraterrestrial. And I eat them – because the little lad keeps staring at me, especially after I groan.

–G'anda wusty!

I even ate half a packet of dried leaves before the daughter told me it was oolong tea.

–It's good for weight loss, she said.

–I don't doubt you, love, I said, and chewed a couple of sardines to help get rid of the taste.

–What in the name of God is whey? I ask her now.

I say it in a way that I hope is closer to David Attenborough than Vincent Browne; I'm aiming for curiosity, not despair. I don't want to hurt her feelings.

–Not sure, she admits. –But it's full of protein, like.

–Grand, I say. –But what is it?

I've a feeling it comes out of the Bible – gold, frankincense and whey. One of the three wise men gave it to Jesus for his birthday. But I might be wrong. And I'm distracted by something else.

–What's that?

It looks like mince.

–Bison, she says.

–What? I say. –Like buffalo?

–Think so.

–Are they not extinct? I ask. –Did John Wayne not kill all of them?

–There's a few left, she says. –They're a great source of protein.

–Now we're talking, I say. –But we'll need a few chips.

I bypass the daughter and go straight to the grandson.

–Will we get some chips?
He nearly passes out.
–Cheee–ips!
Now I look at the daughter.
–What about you, love?
–Ah, yeah, she says. –Go on ahead. Chips are full of—
–Happy fats, I suggest.
She grins.
–Probably.

15

–There's cheese on your chin, Charlie.

–Fake news.

–There is, Charlie, says the wife. –Your fly's wide open.

I grab the zipper and pull.

–The information is true, I tell her. –The news is fake.

I love Trump. He's making my life a lot easier. The fly isn't open; I just hadn't closed it yet. The fact that I'm heading out the front door on my way to a funeral is neither here nor there. The zip is on its way to being closed – big league.

I gave up on buttons about ten years ago. I'd go to open my fly and discover it was already open, and a corner of my shirt sticking out just to advertise the fact – this after battling my way to the jacks through a pub packed with men and women ten, twenty, thirty years younger than me. The fly was open – and it had been like that since the last time I'd gone to the jacks. I finally surrendered when I realised I'd made the same discovery the previous time, the last occasion I'd gone to the jacks. The fly had been open then, I'd gone to the jacks, and forgotten to close it – again.

Shirts weren't the problem; I've never forgotten to button a shirt or a jacket. It was just the trousers – well, the jeans.

Why is that?

Why does old age discriminate against men who wear – or used to wear – jeans with buttons?

Anyway, back then, when I finally admitted to myself that buttons were beyond me, I smuggled the old 501s out of the house – a blue pair and a black pair – when I was bringing the empties to the bottle bank. There's one of those pink clothes recycling bins beside the row of bottle yokes, and that's where they went. It was only two pairs of denim jeans in a plastic bag but I felt like I was shoving my whole life into a black hole.

I cried a bit when I got back into the car.

No, I didn't. But I visit the bottle bank now and again, just to spend a few quiet moments with my former self.

How're you getting on, Charlie?

Well, it's not great in here, to be honest – trapped under bags of unwanted tights and underpants. I expected a bit more of the afterlife.

Anyway.

I rallied. I transferred my allegiance from Levi's to Wranglers and that was grand – a bit of an adventure even, sartorial adultery. It would have helped if someone – anyone – had noticed or given a shite. But, anyway, I soon forgot that I used to forget to button my fly and I had a good eight or nine years when I could stroll through a pub or a wedding, a café or a funeral, safe in the knowledge that my fly would be open only if and when I wanted it to be open. I missed the buttons occasionally. There's an art to buttons; it's something you learn – a bit of a transition from child to adult, from apprentice to craftsman. I mean, any gobshite can use a zip but try opening the buttons on a brand-new pair of Levi 501s when you've four or five pints inside you and the lights in the jacks aren't working. It's the nearest most of us get to going over the top, and not all of us make it back alive.

Anyway, giving up on the buttons was heartbreaking but forgetting the zip is absolutely terrifying. I mean, what's next? Do I become the man who spends the rest of his life in tracksuit bottoms, wandering around Woodie's with his hands down the front of them and his mouth wide open? It's like knocking on heaven's door, except I'm afraid I'll forget to knock. I'll stand outside heaven with my hands down my tracksuit bottoms, staring at the door – for eternity.

Then Trump came along and taught me how to grow old.

Deny.

–Where are the car keys, Charlie?

–On the hook – where I always put them.

–No, they're not there.

–Well, that's the information I was given.

Deny everything. Trump gets away with it. You can see it in his face if you're looking carefully – the panic. Any man who has gone to open his fly and discovered it's already open knows that expression. You can see it when he's walking ahead of Melania. That's not arrogance or misogyny. It's 'Who's your woman! And why is she following me?' Just when the poor lad should be climbing into his final tracksuit he's somehow managed to become the President of the United States.

But he's discovered the way to cope. Deny. Everything. For the next four years.

–You said you'd put out the black wheelie, Charlie.

–I never said that.
–You did.
–No.
–You've a head like a sieve.
–Fake news.

16

The wife sees my face. She knows I'm going to shout at the radio, so she gets there ahead of me.

–Blow it out your arse, love, she says to the voice we've been listening to.

But she doesn't shout. She just talks as if the twit on the radio is with us in the kitchen and she leans across and turns it off. The woman has style.

–Would you like a few Jaffa Cakes with your tea, Charlie? she asks.

This isn't normal. If I want a Jaffa Cake, or anything else, it's up to me to go foraging. And I don't mind that. In fact, I welcome it. I can feel like Robinson Crusoe or Bear Grylls while I'm searching the presses for something worth eating that isn't good for me.

And that's the point: that's why the wife has just offered me chocolate and sponge and orange goo. We've been listening to an expert – a doctor. She's always on the radio and the telly. She's foreign too, so that allows her to give out about the eating habits of the Irish, because in the country she comes from they only eat cabbage and blueberries and they're all as skinny as pipe-cleaners.

Anyway, she's waffling on about the Irish always 'snacking', and how a latte and a muffin – the traditional

Irish snack, by the way, going right back to the days when Oliver Cromwell came over and tried to stop us snacking. The latte and the muffin contain more than seven hundred calories, and the Irish won't stop at one muffin but keep on snacking all day, and that is why we are 'obese'.

That's when I'm getting ready to shout at the radio.

—We're out of luck, the wife says now. —No Jaffa Cakes. Someone found my stash.

There isn't a biscuit or a cake in the house, so we get dug into a block of marzipan left over from a few Christmases ago. It's eighteen months past its best-before date but I'm forty years past mine, so I'm willing to take the risk.

—What is a calorie, anyway? I ask the wife, after we've demolished about half the block.

—A little pain in the arse, she says. —Will we have a glass of sherry with this?

It's ten in the morning, too early for beer.

—I'll get it, I say.

—The bottle's on top of the fridge, she says. —Safe from the little ones.

Nothing's safe from the little ones – the grandkids. We even found them in the basement once – and we don't have a basement. They were digging one, right under the house. They'd made it as far as the Malahide Road by the time I noticed my shovel was missing.

Anyway, we're sipping away, being irresponsibly Irish. We have the house to ourselves; even the dogs are quiet and ignoring the world.

—What's her name, anyway? I ask.

—Who?

—Your one on the radio, I say. —The expert.

—Dr Eva.

–Well, I say, –she could do with a few pints and a packet of cheese and onion.

I don't remember experts on the radio when I was a kid. There were just people who knew a bit more than the rest of us. There was a man who used to read out the prices of cattle. Friesians and Charolais – cows that sounded like American cars. He'd list them off like a poet – the marts, the breeds, the price per hundred-weight. But he wasn't what you'd call an expert. He was just a chap who knew his cows.

I don't know when the experts arrived; I didn't notice. Now, every show has to have at least one of them, every day. A fitness expert, a financial expert, a holiday expert – a gang of chancers and know-alls, all telling us there's only one true path.

But the ones who really get on my wick are the doctors.

–That word, 'obese', I say now.

–What about it?

–What happened to all the other words? I ask.

–Like 'chubby', says the wife.

–Exactly, I say. –And 'plump'.

–Nice words, she says. –'Pleasantly plump.'

–Even 'stout', I say. –A stout man can be attractive.

–And a woman.

–Definitely, I say.

–'Ample', says the wife. –Would you object to a woman described as 'ample', Charlie?

–God, no – never. Or 'well upholstered'.

–A 'big' man, she says.

–Or a 'fine' girl, I say.

–There used to be a word to suit every shape, says the wife, and she pushes the last bit of marzipan over to me.

I push it back – enough is enough.

–Then the doctors take over the radio, I say. –And all of a sudden we go straight from thin to obese – there's nothing in the middle.

–You're either perfect or a disaster.

I lift my sherry.

–Well, I'm with the disasters.

–Hear hear, she says. –What're you doing later?

–Gym and a few pints.

–Lovely.

17

We're having a bit of a family dinner – the wife and her two sisters, a husband and a partner, and myself. The partner is new-ish. I'm not sure if he's even the partner or still just the boyfriend; I don't really know when one thing ends and the other thing starts. But it feels a bit odd to be calling a bald man with a brand new hip the boyfriend. So, partner it is.

Anyway, it's a kid-and-grandkid-free zone for the evening, so the crack is good and the food – Carmel's famous *chilli con carne y rashers* – is dynamite.

Paddy, Carmel's husband, is sound. I've always liked him. He has one of those faces. He doesn't have to talk – although he does, a lot. But Paddy can express things with his eyebrows that would take the rest of us thousands of words. It's one of those big, loose faces. And it's always been like that. I've known Paddy since he was nineteen and his face has always been a bit spectacular, or arresting. But I'm probably not doing him justice; I've been told he's a handsome man.

Now that I think of it, it was Paddy himself who told me that.

Anyway, we're sitting around the table when the youngest sister's partner announces that he's off to Prague in a couple of weeks.

–Death or teeth? says Paddy.

–What?

–That's why you'd go to Prague, isn't it? says Paddy. –Either you're getting the teeth done cos it's too expensive here, or you're having a gawk at Prague because it's on your bucket list.

–My daughter lives there, says the partner.

–Oh, says Paddy. –Grand. Give her my regards. It's funny but, isn't it? The bucket list thing.

And that gets us going.

You find out you're dying and, seconds later, before you're over the shock – before you've even had time to be shocked – you sit down and start writing out a list of the things you want to do, the places you want to see, before you kick the bucket. And, while all of us agree that the whole idea is daft, Carmel finds a pen and tears the back off the cornflakes box and we get motoring on our list.

And it's boring – it's really boring.

–Hands on the hearts now, says Paddy. –Could you really give a shite about seeing the Taj Mahal?

I don't have to put my hand on my heart.

–No, I say. –All it would do is remind me that I'm dying.

–Because that's the only reason you'd be standing in front of it in the first place?

–Yeah.

–No, says Carmel. –I really want to see it.

–So, why don't you? While you're healthy.

She shrugs.

–Too far, she says.

We go through the list and admit that we couldn't really be arsed going to any of these places. Kilimanjaro, Table Mountain, Timbuktu, Rio, Bombay, the Amazon, the Arctic, Ballybunion – we put a line through everything.

–Are we happy enough where we are, so?

–No.

–It can't be just places, says the wife. –You don't live your life just so you can see Niagara Falls.

–What then, love? I ask her. –What should we do? What *is* our purpose in life?

–Ah, Jaysis, says Paddy. –What have I started?

The women leave before we can go too deep into the philosophy because their band, the Pelvic Floors, have a late-night gig in the Workman's, on Wellington Quay.

–So, lads, says Paddy, after he hears the front door closing.–We don't really want to climb Everest or see the Swinging Gardens of Fort Apache.

–Nope.

–We need a new list, he says.

He picks up the pen.

–Sophia Loren, he says, and he slowly writes the name on the cardboard.

–I think she's dead, says the partner.

–She's not, is she?

–I think so, yeah.

–I don't care, says Paddy. –She's on the list.

–Hang on, Paddy, I say.

I don't normally like googling. There's nothing worse than the bore who takes out his phone when you're all having a great time trying to remember the names of all the players who played for both Liverpool *and* Everton. But this is Sophia Loren we're talking about.

I look up from the phone.

–She's alive, I tell them.

–Brilliant, says Paddy. –That's a relief.

–She was born in 1934.

–Grand, says Paddy.

I do the sums.

–She's eighty-three, I say.

–Yeah, says Paddy. –So?

He stares at me. An eyebrow rises, and falls.

–Right, he says. –This is what I'm writing. *Sophia Loren 1958.*

–Hang on, I say. –What age were you in 1958?

–Six, says Paddy.

–This isn't a bucket list, Paddy, I protest. –It's a different kind of list altogether.

He stares at me again. The eyebrow rises, and stays up there.

–Make your own bleedin' list then, he says.

And that's where the problems start – because I do.

18

I haven't been down to the local in a while. Various reasons: a bad cold, a broken tooth, determination to get through all of Season 6 of *Homeland* without anyone telling me what happens. But I'm there now – in the local – and I'm sitting beside my pal, the Secret Woman.

–Do you have a bucket list? I ask him.

He surprises me.

–Yeah, he says. –I do.

–Do you, really?

–I just told you I did.

–What's on it? I ask him.

–A bucket.

–What?

–A bucket, he says again. –I need a new one.

He picks up his pint.

–And a trowel, he says.

–Jesus, I say. –For a man who secretly yearns to be a woman you're a bitter disappointment.

–Listen, Charlie, he says. –I'll just say this and then we can move on to the football. After my wife died, the only thing I wanted was for her to come back. But she didn't and she couldn't. But it's still the only thing

68

that'll ever be on my bucket list and it's never going to happen. What about you?

–What about me? I say.

I'm such a dope, such an insensitive eejit – talking about death and bucket lists with a man who's been grieving in front of me for the last two years.

–What's on your list? he asks.

–Ah, nothing, I say.

–No, go on, he says. –Tell me.

–Well, I say. –I wouldn't mind going to Shelbourne Park.

–To the dog racing?

–Yeah, I say. –Exactly.

–Why don't you? he says. –I'll come with you.

–Because, I say. –This sounds stupid now. I'd be afraid I'd die.

I've never been superstitious. At least, I didn't know I was. I've broken a few mirrors in my day and it's never worried me. Except that one time when it was my forehead that broke the glass – but that's a different story. I've never minded stepping on cracks in the pavement and I regularly open umbrellas inside the house – when I'm playing Mary Poppins with the grandkids and it's my turn to be Mary. I proposed to the wife on Friday the 13th, standing under a ladder. At least, she was standing under it. So maybe she got the bad luck.

I won't be asking her.

Anyway. The point is, I've never been superstitious. But ever since we started compiling our bucket list – myself and the wife and her sisters and the husband and the partner – I've been feeling a pain in my chest. Or, the threat of a pain. Even though it was only a bit of crack and we soon got bored with it.

I can't get the bucket list out of my head.

–That's madness, Charlie, says the Secret Woman, after I tell him why the greyhounds frighten me.

–I know, I say. –It's daft – I know.

The bloody bucket list.

I lie awake half the night, worrying. Waiting. For the heart attack or the stroke. It's beating away, like a drum in a room down the hall.

–What else is on the list? the Secret Woman asks.

–I'd like to paint, I tell him.

–Pictures?

–Yeah, I lie. –I've always wanted to paint.

It just came into my head. I've never thought about painting – not even when I was doing art in school. I'd paint an apple and an orange and a vase – I think it was called a still life – and I'd think about Saturday's football and the young one who worked behind the counter in the Mint – but never about the paint.

–A night class? says the Secret Woman. –Is that what you want?

–Kind of, I say. –Yeah.

Here is a list – another bloody list – of the very last things I'd want: a nuclear war, a bad dose of leprosy, a night class.

I blame Paddy, the brother-in-law.

It was harmless enough while we were just making a list of the places we'd like to see. But when he changed it – when he wrote 'Sophia Loren', I realised something. The bucket list isn't about wishes; it's actually about regret.

'Regrets I've had a few but, then again, too few to mention – *out loud*.' That's what Frank Sinatra should have sung if he'd wanted to be honest.

Don't get me wrong. I don't for a second think I'd ever have had a chance with Sophia Loren, even if she'd lived on our road. 'Here – Sophia! Charlie Savage wants to know if you'll go with him.' But back then, when I was a kid, I had my own Sophia. She worked in the Mint after school and her name was Eileen Pidgeon.

–What else is on your list? the Secret Woman asks me.

–Well, I say.

I take a breath. The heart is hopping.

–There was this girl.

–Ah, Jesus, Charlie, no, he says.

I shake my head.

–Too late, I say. –I'm meeting her on Friday.

19

I blame Facebook.

1990: A man well into his autumn years remembers a young woman who won, and broke, his heart when he was sixteen and he wonders what she's like now – and he keeps on wondering, now and again, until he hits the far end of the winter years, and dies.

2017: A man in his autumn years remembers a young woman who broke his heart when he was sixteen and wonders what she's like now – and looks her up on bloody Facebook, and finds her.

–Jesus, Charlie, says the Secret Woman when I tell him that I'm after arranging to meet Eileen.

–I know, I say. –I know.

–What sort of a gobshite are you? he says.

–A complete and utter one, I say.

–Bang on, he says. –What happened?

–Well, I say. –I think I pressed the wrong yoke.

Eileen Pidgeon was my girlfriend when I was sixteen, not far off fifty years ago. I held her hand twice and kissed her once. My eyes were shut at the time and I've a feeling I missed her mouth. I think now, looking back over the decades, that I was kissing Eileen's cheek-bone, wondering where her tongue was, and that the wet sensation on my chin was Eileen's tongue wondering where my mouth was. I slid my hand in under her jumper as well, but I'm not sure if I trust that memory either. If I'm being honest, my hand might have gone under my own jumper.

But anyway. We went our separate ways soon after – later that same day, actually – when I found her behind the coal shed with my brother Pat. She broke my heart, that young one. She also left a fair-sized dent in my self-respect because Pat was a year and a half younger than me and he had to stand on an inverted coal bucket to – very successfully – reach Eileen's mouth.

Now, out of nowhere, she's become the love of my life – my one huge regret. A month ago, I couldn't even remember her name.

God, I'm such an eejit.

I even phoned Pat – the little brother – to see if he could remember the girl's name. But he claimed he couldn't remember any girl and he even denied we'd ever had a coal shed.

–Jesus, Pat, where do you think we kept the coal? I said.

–Was it not under the bed?

–No!

But the call left me rattled. I couldn't remember the coal shed now, myself, even though I definitely remember finding Pat behind it, with the love of my life wrapped around him. It made me wonder if I could trust any of my memories. I could remember the look on Pat's face when I caught him, looking over her shoulder back at me. But then, that was the look he always had – because he was always getting caught. It was why he joined the Guards, so he could do the catching instead.

73

Anyway.

–You eventually remembered her name, the Secret Woman reminds me now.

–Yeah.

–Eileen Pidgeon, he says.

–Yeah.

–And you looked her up on Facebook, he says.

–Yeah.

–And there she was – on Facebook, he says.

–Yeah.

–Charlie, he says.

–What?

–You're the one that's supposed to be telling the story, he says. –But I'm doing all the work.

–Sorry, I say. –So, yeah. So, then I pressed the wrong yoke.

–What do you mean?

–I meant to have a look at her photos, I say. –Cos the photo in the top corner wasn't a picture of her. It was a bunch of flowers.

–What did you press? he asks.

–Well, I was on my sweeney in the kitchen, I say. –For once. And I'm just going to have a quick gawk at her snaps when some of the grandkids charge in and I kind of panicked and pressed the 'Add friend' button instead.

–Brilliant, he says. –What happened then?

–I got a message.

–On Facebook?

–A few days later – yeah.

–From Eileen?

–Yeah, I say. –Like a voice from the dead.

–Brilliant, he says – again.

He's having the time of his life, listening. And, actually, that makes me start to enjoy myself, telling him.

–'Is that you, Charlie Savage?' I say.

–Was that the whole message?

–Every word.

–It's a bit – I don't know – spooky, he says. –Isn't it?

–I thought so, yeah.

–Did you answer?

–'Is that you, Eileen Pidgeon?'

–I never knew you were such a flirt, Charlie, he says.

–I couldn't think of anything else, I say. –I wasn't bloody flirting – I don't think I was.

–But you're meeting her.

–Yeah.

I look at him now.

–Will you do me a favour? I ask him.

–What?

–Come with me.

–No way, he says.

But, even as he says it, I can see him changing his mind.

–Okay, he says.

He grins.

–Can't wait.

20

We're on the Dart to Greystones, me and my pal, the Secret Woman. I'm on my way to meet Eileen Pidgeon. I really don't know why I'm doing this, and that's the honest to God truth – I think. The Secret Woman is here to hold my hand, although he's not actually holding my hand and has made no attempt to hold it. He's sitting beside me with his head – his whole body – pushed forward, like a child trying to make the train go faster.

–Why Greystones, by the way? he asks. –Does she live there?

–No, I say.

I look around to make sure there's no one earwigging.

–She lives in Navan, I tell him.

–And you're meeting her in Greystones? he says. – Why not go the whole hog and meet her in Mexico City or one of the Aran Islands?

He's much more sarcastic than he used to be, before he decided he wanted to be a woman.

I ignore him.

No, I don't.

–You're fuckin' hilarious, I tell him.

He's looking up at the map of the stations, above the window. We're at Connolly.

–Eighteen stops, he says. –Just seventeen more opportunities to change your mind.

He's not being sarcastic now.

–And come here, he says. –I won't think any less of you if you do.

–Thanks, I say.

–Although I'd be a bit disappointed, he adds.

–Okay.

What happens to the brain? Is there a microbe or a parasite that gets in there and eats the wiring? I'm a happily married man. I really am. Yet I'm heading towards some sort of disaster, and I'm even paying my own fare. (I'm a few years off the free travel but I didn't want to wait.) The Dart's only bringing me to Greystones; it's not bringing me back forty-seven years to that moment when I caught Eileen and my little brother wearing the faces off each other – or, to the moment just before that moment.

I don't think I'm living in *Back to the Future* or – what's the name of that one where Arnold Schwarzenegger goes back in time to change history? Well, I'm not in that one either. I'm not heading to Greystones to change the course of history. I'm only going for a coffee and a scone and a chat. With an elderly woman who was a girl the last time I gazed at her with lovestruck eyes.

Ah, Jesus.

The Secret Woman is looking up at the map again.

–Ten stops, Charlie.

–Shut up.

–Only saying.

Terminator – that was the name of it. And he did manage to change history, if I'm remembering it right.

But I'm not Arnie and changing my socks is a big enough challenge, never mind bloody history.

What gets into us? What's got into *me*? We're living too long. That's my theory – today.

–Seven stops.

–Thanks.

–The rain's staying away, anyway.

–Yep.

–We should've brought the clubs.

He's having another dig at me. I told the wife I was heading off to play pitch and putt and I left my putter and 8-iron – Exhibits A and B, he called them – in the Secret Woman's house, before we dashed for the Dart.

It used to be, we'd retire, live a few years and die. The odd man and woman made it into the late seventies and eighties; it was like a job – the village crone or the 1916 veteran. The rest of us were dead and buried before we could start causing mischief. *Idle hands are the Devil's workshop.* And it doesn't matter how old and arthritic the hands are.

Bloody bucket lists.

–Four stops, Charlie.

–Your mathematical ability never fails to astonish me.

–Doesn't the sea look glorious, all the same?

–It does.

–We should've brought the togs.

–Have you bought a bikini yet?

–Not funny.

–Sorry – you're right.

–Okay, he says. –Three stops, by the way.

I don't want this to happen. I really do not want this to happen. I've been saying it in my head for weeks: I'm a happily married man, I'm a happily married man. Regret is desperate; it's worse than cancer or haemorrhoids. Sinatra was a young man when he recorded *My Way*. He was only fifty-three, and I'm betting he hated the stupid song by the time he hit sixty-three.

–Two stops, Charlie. You are entering the Last Chance Saloon.

A thought hits me: What if the wife's doing the same thing? Looking for old boyfriends, scouring through Facebook, imagining a time before she strayed into Jurassic Park and met me.

Ah, Jesus.

–We're here, says the Secret Woman.

He hasn't sounded this happy since Snow White woke up. He grabs my shoulder and helps me out of the station.

There's no one here, no woman waiting. I'm so relieved – so relieved and devastated.

There's a voice behind me.

–Charlie?

21

I'm outside Greystones Dart station. I'm with my pal, the Secret Woman, but I'm there to meet Eileen Pidgeon and it looks like she hasn't turned up. I'm relieved, to be honest – but a bit hurt too. I've come twenty-four stops on the Dart. I haven't been this far south since myself and the wife went to the Algarve ten years ago. I don't mind not meeting Eileen – I really don't. But at the same time, I've been dying to see her, to see her as she is now, nearly fifty years after she dumped me for my little brother.

We hear a voice.

–Charlie?

It's a woman, behind us. She's just spoken my name but she's looking at the Secret Woman.

–Charlie? she says again – she's smiling.

He points at me.

–That's him there, he says.

–Oh, she says.

–How's it going, Eileen? I say.

–Fine, she says. –Not too bad. So, is this Pat then?

She's still looking at the Secret Woman and she's wondering if he's my brother Pat.

–No, he tells her. –I'm just a friend of Charlie's.

–Oh.

–They let him out for the day, I tell her, and we all laugh – eventually.

She's looking well – I'll say that. She's looking very well. My memory hasn't let me down; the younger version of the woman in front of me must have been well worth the misery. And her smile – Jaysis – it's fighting the Greystones gloom and winning. I'm glad I remembered to wear my Jamie Redknapp shirt.

–Isn't this mad? she says.

–It is a bit, I say. –But no harm.

–No, she agrees.

We walk deeper into the town – not that there's much of it. Eileen walks beside me and the Secret Woman is kind of behind us, except where the path is wider, when he can walk on the other side of Eileen.

She's a widow, she tells me. She has been since she was thirty-two.

–What happened?

–He died, she says.

–Oh.

She has a son who lives in Perth. She takes out her phone to show me the grandkids. I can't make them out without my reading glasses but I pretend they're lovely and give the phone back to her.

I give her my story – the wife, the kids, the grandkids. I don't show her photos. I'm not sure why not.

We're passing some sort of a café – the Happy Pear, it's called.

–D'you fancy a coffee or a cuppa, Eileen? I ask her.

–It's a vegetarian place, is it? she says. –I wouldn't trust the tea you'd get in there.

Then she laughs, and we both laugh with her. She's gas – she's lovely. She's lovely, and I just want to go

81

home. The thirty years of widowhood, the grandkids so far away – I'm falling in love with the sadness. I feel like I've never really lived.

We come to another café, so in we go. She asks for tea and myself and the Secret Woman opt for coffee and a couple of the big scones.

Eileen nods at one of the scones.

–Are you supposed to eat it or climb it? she asks, and that has us howling again. *Don't get jam on your shirt, don't get jam on your shirt*, I keep telling myself – and I see that the Secret Woman already has jam on his, and that makes me ludicrously happy.

I'm telling Eileen about my SpongeBob tattoo and I can see she's loving the story when I realise I'm going to have to get up and go to the toilet.

It's just as well all the great stories are about young people, with young bladders. Can you imagine what the end of *Casablanca* would have been like if Humphrey Bogart had been twenty years older? 'If that plane leaves the ground and you're not with him, you'll regret it. Maybe not today, maybe not – hang on, love, I'll be back in a minute.' Or if Jesus had been sixty-three not thirty-three. Instead of 'Jesus falls the second time', it would have been 'Jesus has to go to the jacks the fourth time.' Christianity would never have taken off.

But anyway. I go to the jacks, wash the hands, check the shirt and eyebrows, make sure I shaved SpongeBob the night before, and go back out.

And Eileen's kissing the Secret Woman. Or, they have been kissing – I can tell. The look on their faces – the redners. They've been holding hands as well, across the table.

I look straight at her.

–Again!

I look at the Secret Woman.

–And you! I say. –You fuckin' traitor! You told me you weren't a lesbian.

And I storm out.

Storming out is something no man in his sixties should ever do, but I do it anyway – I even slam the door. I'm halfway back down to the station when I realise I'm happy. I've escaped. I'm going home.

22

I like my football. And I've noticed recently, the wife likes my football too. And, believe me, that hasn't always been the case.

When she found out, when we started going out – this is forty years back – that my reluctance to meet her on Saturday nights was down to the fact that I was staying in to watch *Match of the Day*, well, she wasn't happy. (This was before videos, by the way.) I'd told her I had to work on Saturday nights but she copped on when I made myself available at the end of the season.

–D'you not have to work on Saturdays?

–No, I said. –Not any more.

–How come?

It's an evil question, when you think about it. It looks harmless enough but that little question – *How come?* – has brought down empires. And I'll just say this and leave it at that: I've never heard a man ask it.

Anyway. The question caught me – like millions of other lads – on the hop. I couldn't think of anything, except the honest answer – and I wasn't going to give her that. But I could see her flicking through her mental filing cabinet, and finding the answer herself.

–My God, she said. –*Match of the* bloody *Day*.

I said nothing.

–Am I right?

–Well, yeah, I said. –But my da's going blind, so I have to tell him what's happening.

I'd forgotten: she'd met my da. He'd told her she was gorgeous, so she was never going to accept that he was blind. (He wasn't and, even if he was, there was always John Motson to tell him what was happening.)

I remember her staring at my Man United jersey. We were going to her little brother's confirmation, so I probably should have worn something a bit more formal.

–Well, Charlie, she said. –Who's it to be? Me or Lou Macari?

I couldn't decide if she was going to walk away or clatter me, but she was definitely going to do something. So—

–You, I said.

And we all lived happily ever after.

Anyway. The best thing about having kids is that your life is over. You stop going out, you lose your friends, you forget how to sleep – and you get to stay in and watch *Match of the Day*. I just have to hear the music and I feel such overwhelming love for my children, the legs go from under me and I have to sit in front of the telly. John Travolta's face at the start of *Saturday Night Fever*, when he's walking down the street in his suit, with the can of paint – you can tell: he's on his way home to watch *Match of the Day*.

I've had *Match of the Day* – or *MOTD*, as the busy people call it these days – all to myself, for decades.

Until recently.

At this end of my life 'recently' means nine or ten years. But I can be more exact. The wife often sat beside me while *Match of the Day* was on but she started actually watching it thirteen years ago – in August 2004, to be exact.

Fuckin' Mourinho.

–Who's that? she asked.

–Who?

–The good-looking one.

–What good-looking one?

In my innocence I thought she was asking about one of the twenty–two players on the pitch. But it was José Mourinho who'd impressed her.

And fair enough. The stats spoke for themselves. But so, she told me, did his eyes, his suit, his accent and his smile. And the technology had arrived with him; she kept telling me to pause and go back, so we could see him scowl again, or grin again, or poke some poor innocent fucker in the eye again.

–He's gas, she said.

–He's a psychopath.

–Yeah, she agreed – and sighed.

Mourinho left for a while but other good-looking Continental men who wore clothes that fit them arrived and took over the telly. Now, when I'm watching a match, I'm actually watching Conte or Klopp or Pep Guardiola, and the occasional footballer kicking a ball. I'm exaggerating a bit, but only a bit.

But the thing is: she loves the football. And I never noticed.

I only realised it a few weeks ago when I put on Burnley v. Crystal Palace and sat back to see how she'd react, because both teams are managed by pasty-faced Englishmen who get their clothes from a skip behind the local Oxfam shop. I couldn't wait to see her face.

–Who's playing? she asked.

I told her.

–Brilliant, she said, and sat down. –This'll be a real battle. Is Robbie Brady playing, is he?

It's weird – it's worrying. As the game went on, she was wondering why Burnley didn't play three at the back and I was wondering why Crystal Palace's manager, Sam Allardyce, couldn't find a shirt that fit him properly.

23

I dread the summer.

I mean, I don't mind the sun – when there is one – or the longer days. I don't mind the holidays; I've no objection to being buried to my neck in sand by the grandkids, just as long as they remember to come back and dig me out before the tide comes in. And, in fairness, they do remember – more often than not.

We've a mobile in Wexford, near Kilmuckridge, and the whole new potatoes and strawberries hysteria down there gets on my wick. I'm always half-terrified I'm going to run over some young one or young lad selling the things on the side of the road. And the gobshites who veer off the road at the mere sight of a punnet of strawberries or a jar of jam – don't get me started on those clowns.

But I always like it down there, regardless of the weather, and by the time I've put the shorts on and hosed the squashed strawberry seller off the front bumper, I'm a happy enough camper.

But there's always something missing: the football.

It starts before the summer arrives – the grief. The last few matches of the season in late April and May are a bit like visits to the hospital to see a loved one who's on the way out. Every final whistle is bringing you closer to the *final* whistle.

I wake up every Saturday knowing it's Saturday – and it's often the only thing I know. Who am I, where am I, *what* am I? These questions get answered later – quite quickly, in fact. By the time I'm on my way down the stairs to the kettle I generally know who and where I am. *What* I am has to wait till after the coffee.

But the one big thought is there from the start, before I'm fully conscious: football. And it's been like that since I was a child. Saturday is football. I know, there's football on Sundays too these days, and Mondays, Tuesdays, Wednesdays – every day of the week and every hour of the day. But Saturday is still *the* football day, even if your team is playing the day after. I worked most Saturdays when I was a young lad and I still loved waking up on Saturday.

I once woke up in a ditch in Wales – it's a long story. I'd no idea where I was but I knew it was Saturday. It was raining, I'd no shoes or sterling – but I was still happy. I was out in the middle of nowhere, in a different jurisdiction, with a hangover that felt like most of the Second World War but I knew I'd make it to a radio in time for the final results. That was way more important than getting back to Ireland in time for the wedding – *my* wedding.

Anyway. There's no football in the summer and it's a struggle. I'm told that old people dread the winter. They haven't a clue. I'm old now, myself – so the daughter says. *You're in the prime of your decline, Dad, and you should make the most of it; it's a fabulous opportunity, like.* The hardships of winter, the cold, the ice, the hypothermia, the darkness, the *Late Late Show*? Bring them on. It's the summer that's going to kill me.

I was watching a match a few weeks ago. I had the grandson, the daughter's little lad, on my knee. I had the wife beside me. We had the dogs in front of us. I usually let them in for the live games because they bark at the referee and it's always – always – a laugh.

The grandson's barely three but he already loves his football. I have him well trained. When the camera homes in on a Man United player he looks up at me.

–B'illi'nt? (That's 'brilliant' to you and me.)

–Yes, love, I say.

Any other player – anyone dressed in blue, black, stripes or that strange shade of pink worn by Liverpool, he looks up again.

–Hobs'ite? (That's 'gobshite', by the way.)

–Yes, love.

It's wonderful – it's almost miraculous, witnessing the child's development, particularly his flair for language. And there's a moment I'll never forget. One of the United players, Marouane Fellaini, has just been sent off for head-butting an opponent. It's shocking – even the dogs have shut up. Fellaini's face – *Who, me?* – fills the screen.

The little lad tugs at my trouser leg.

–Hobs'ite? he asks.

I'm stunned. Like the dogs, I'm speechless.

He's just asked me to confirm that one of his own players is a gobshite. He's become – right there on my knee – a true football man. In the company of his grandad and his nanny – a football woman – and the dogs.

This is domestic bliss. This is why I live.

And this is what I lose in the summer.

24

I'm under attack from both flanks, in one of those pincer movements that were very popular during the Second World War.

It's probably not fair to refer to my wife and daughter as 'flanks' and, strictly speaking, I'm not under attack at all. But I still feel that my whole way of life – or, more accurately, my lack of a way of life – is under threat. I'm determined to resist but I know I'll give in. My days are numbered.

It's my own fault. I should never have said it. Here's what I said:

–I've nothing to do.

It's not so much that I said it. It's more *how* I said it, the context. I walked into the kitchen and—

–I've nothing to do, I said.

I wasn't answering a question or taking part in a conversation about the meaning of life. It just popped, as they say, out.

–I've nothing to do.

–You could cut the grass, said the wife, but she was being sarcastic. We don't have any grass – the dogs have seen to that. The back garden no longer exists. Where there used to be grass and flowers, an apple tree and a trampoline, there is now a collection of holes in the ground – and shite. There isn't a blade of grass or the remains of a hedge out there. I think they even ate the trampoline.

Anyway. The wife looks at me and she must see something. I haven't a clue what it might be because my facial expression hasn't changed since October 1998 – or so I'm told.

Anyway, she suddenly looks concerned. It's not the look a virile man wants to see on the face of the woman standing in front of him. Give me anger any day – or even bafflement. But the Princess Diana 'Battered This, Battered That' mush? I just want to go outside and dig a new hole with the dogs.

Anyway.

–Charlie, she says. –What's wrong?

–Ah, nothing, I say.

My second mistake. I should just have said, 'Nothing'. But I said, 'Ah, nothing.' And the 'Ah' in front of 'nothing' changes the meaning of the word, completely. 'Nothing' becomes 'something', 'a lot', 'everything'. I might as well have told her, 'My life is falling apart at the seams' – or where there used to be seams. Her facial expression: she looks like a very attractive mother superior gazing at a leper.

And the daughter walks in.

–What's wrong?

I can't tell them the truth. Which is simple – but dare not speak its name.

I can't go to the pub.

Not since my pal, the Secret Woman, got off with my old girlfriend, Eileen Pidgeon, in a café in Greystones while I was out in the jacks. I'm ready to forgive the man – he was probably doing me some kind of an accidental favour. But I'm afraid – terrified – I'll find Eileen sitting on my stool, her arse parked where my arse should be, up at the bar, to the left of the Guinness tap.

I can't tell them – the wife and the daughter – that the local is out of bounds. I could, but then I'd have to tell them that I'd had a row with my pal. And one of them or both of them would ask, 'What about?', and I can hear myself saying it again – 'Ah, nothing'.

I love them both dearly – so, so, *so* much – but the KGB and the Gestapo had nothing on the women in my life when it comes to extracting information. Torture isn't necessary, not even the threat of it. They just have to look at me. They don't even have to look; I just have to know they're going to.

So I tell a lie.

–There's no football on.

It's not really a lie – or not a whopper, anyway. There actually isn't any football on. The season's over and the summer yawns in front of me. Tennis, cricket, the GAA, fresh air, good cheer, bronzed bodies – I hate every minute of it. I pine for the dark of winter and the offside trap.

But the lack of football isn't why I'm moping around the house just now, when the sun is sliding behind the back wall and I should be thinking about migrating to the pub. But I can't tell them the truth: I'm scared Eileen Pidgeon will be there. The questions, the consequences, the absurdity – I couldn't cope; western democracy couldn't cope. It's my duty to lie.

–There's no football on.

And it works.

Kind of.

–Ah, for Christ's sake – Charlie! I thought you had cancer!

–Ah, Dad – get a grip, like.

The wife's forgotten that a few minutes ago I looked like mankind on the brink of extinction. Now, she's just looking at an eejit, an elderly brat. The daughter, however, is looking at a project.

And I'm doomed.

25

I've never been a lazy man. I worked hard all my life, when I had to. I played a vigorous game of football until I didn't want to – when I was thirty-four. I wasn't very good but no one else was either, except for one chap who went on to nearly play for Bohs. I gave it my all – or most of my all – until I realised that the little bastard running past me was sixteen years younger than me and didn't have five kids. So, the next time he was in my vicinity – about half an hour later – I gave him a kick, got sent off, told the ref he was only a Cabra bollix, and hung up my boots, in that order.

My point is: I'm not lazy but I'm realistic. If something needs doing I'll do it. But I'm the one who'll decide if it needs doing. Unless it's the wife or the daughter who decide; then I'll hop to it and do exactly what I'm told. After the futile, token resistance.

–You could do with a haircut, Dad.

–My hair's grand – leave it alone.

–You look like that mad fella – Einstein, like.

–Einstein was a genius, I tell her. –I'm just happy to have hair.

–But that's the point, like, she says. –You should be using it to your advantage but I look at you, Dad, and I see a man who's being bullied by his hair.

I've no idea what she's talking about. But I trot down to the barber. It's either that or she'll do the job herself and I'll end up looking like a boy-band member who's been lost in his dressing room for the last fifty years.

I bring some of the dogs for the occasional walk, around the block or sometimes as far as the shopping centre, where I let them piss against the window of Insomnia, and come home. It's a small act of revenge: about three years ago, a young lad behind the counter raised his eyes to heaven when I asked him for 'a plain black coffee with no messing'. He's long gone but the dogs are so well trained, they piss at the sight of the Insomnia logo, so I can't stop them.

Anyway, somehow or other the walk became some sort of a scientific experiment. The daughter times me, to the nanosecond, and even factors in the age, weight and number of the dogs that are dragging me down the road. It's my health she's looking after but she's murdering the dogs.

Moving on.

I'm no stranger to the inside of the dishwasher, and the washing machine actually hums when it sees me approaching; we've become quite close over the years. I do my fair share, is what I'm saying. And the wife wouldn't disagree with me. The daughter has grown up eating grub I've cooked and wearing clothes I've shrunk. If there can be gods that are just fair enough, then I'm a domestic god.

So I know – and they know: they're not at me because they think I'm useless. When I walked into the kitchen a week ago and complained – well, whinged – that I'd nothing to do, the wife was exasperated. She's reared her kids and she doesn't want to start all over again, rearing a cranky, elderly infant. There's already one of them in charge of the free world, so she doesn't want another one in the house, in charge of the dishes.

But she wasn't just being impatient. She was worried.

And so is the daughter.

They don't like seeing me getting older. I don't see it, because I don't have to look at myself that often and I've started taking my glasses off whenever I'm near the bathroom mirror.

Anyway, when I see them looking at me, and at each other, and back at me, I know they're going to force me back into the tracksuit I'd shoved under the bed, and make me climb mountains and eat vegetables I can't pronounce.

But I'm wrong.

They say nothing. They retreat. They leave me alone in the kitchen – with nothing to do.

One thing I don't really notice at the time: the daughter turns on the radio as she's walking out.

And I shout at it – the radio.

Not immediately. But a few minutes later when the news comes on and there's some eejit going on about Enda Kenny's legacy.

And I shout.

–What legacy, you gobshite?

And they're back in the room – the wife and daughter, but especially the daughter, if that makes sense.

She turns off the radio.

–Dad, she says.

–What?

–You're going to have to do more than just keep calling the radio a gobshite, like.

She has the look in the eyes: you are my project.

–You're going to become a social influencer, she says.

26

I'm standing in the kitchen.

The wife and the daughter are with me.

There are 'warm' smiles and 'happy' and 'affection-ate' and 'winning' smiles – but can a smile ever be described as 'determined'? I ask, because they're smiling at me but their eyes are doing something else entirely. They look a bit like a pair of aliens who've been taught how to smile but they haven't quite mastered it yet. The upturned mouths tell me they've come in peace but the eyes tell a different story: they are here to take over my world.

I've been half-expecting this. Now, I don't actually think the wife and the daughter are aliens. What's the name of that book I saw in the wife's sister's house once? *Men Are from Mars, Women Are from Venus*. Well, the wife's from Coolock and it's only a mile up the road.

No, what I've been anticipating is another campaign to get me to change my lifestyle. I've been expecting exercise regimes and dietary demands. They've tried it before and I find that the best policy has always been to go along with it until they forget.

But this time it's different. It's not about broccoli or body fat. The daughter has just told me that I'm going to become a social influencer. I don't know what that means but it doesn't matter; the words – 'social' and 'influencer' – grab my heart like two hands, and squeeze. The answer to the question, 'What in the name of Jaysis is a social influencer?', will more than likely kill me.

And it's my own fault.

The radio was the bait. The daughter had turned it on when she was walking out of the kitchen. She knew I'd shout at it, and I didn't let her down. I come from a long tradition of men who shout at the wireless. It works for telly as well, but the newer media – phones, iPads and what have you – are all useless. Show me a man who shouts at his phone – *at*, not *into* – and I'll show you a nitwit. But one who shouts at the radio? You're looking at a man at ease with his masculinity.

It was my father who taught me how to shout.

–Is he a gobshite, Da?

We were listening to Mícheál O'Hehir criticising the Dubs.

–He is, son – let him have it.

–Gobshite!

–Good man. How did that feel?

–Brilliant.

He taught me when to shout and when to wait, when to stare at the wireless with incredulity and when – and how – to stride across the room and turn it off. And, just the once, he even showed me how to throw it out the window. He shouted at the wireless, even when there was nothing on. My mother asked him why and he answered, 'I know what they're thinking.'

Anyway. My father grew up shouting at De Valera and Churchill – a golden age of shouting. But I shout at everyone – politicians, most football pundits, at virtually everyone on between the hours of nine and midday, and at the bells of the Angelus, all eighteen of them.

—Bong, yourself!

And this, the daughter tells me, makes me qualified to become a social influencer.

I look it up – I google it – I slip on the reading glasses when she's not looking. *A social influencer is someone whose opinions carry more weight with their colleagues and the general public than is the case with most individuals.*

It's drivel, but I'm flattered.

Social influencers establish large followings on social media such as Facebook *and* Twitter *and are widely considered authorities among their followers.*

Oh, Jesus.

She has the wrong man.

I know my mistake. I've been shouting too often, and at too many. I've been shouting at chefs and consultants and style gurus – and everyone. When I roared, 'What would *you* know?' I never meant to suggest – not for a minute – that *I* knew. I'd shout at myself if I heard me on the radio.

I know: they – the wife and daughter – have been worried about me. I went to the GP a few weeks back. He took my blood pressure and told me I was grand but I needed an interest. And I made the mistake of telling them.

And now, apparently, I have one. I'm a social influencer and, unknown to myself, I have been for the past week.

The daughter holds up her iPad and shows me the Facebook page she's designed for me: *The Shouter*. She points at a number.

–You have eighty-seven followers, like.

She shows me a video. It's me – I'm standing in front of the radio. I've just heard Leo Varadkar saying that he represents the people who get up early in the morning.

And I shout.

–That's it, so! I'm staying in bed till the next fuckin' election!

She points at the number.

I have ninety-one followers.

27

Being Ireland's foremost elderly social influencer is a full-time job.

It's all go, from the minute I wake up – earlier than you, Varadkar – to that dog-tired decision at the end of the day, 'Will I bother with my teeth or just brush them really, really hard in the morning?' There isn't a moment in the day that isn't a potential opportunity.

Or so I'm told.

By the daughter.

She has me shouting at everything.

–I'm supposed to be retired, love, I tell her.

–That doesn't mean your brain's retired, Dad, she says.

She's right, of course. But I wish my mouth was – retired, that is. Or even working part-time. When the doctor said he thought I needed an interest, I think he had stamp collecting in mind, or hill walking, or having a go at the garden. I don't think he expected me to go home and start shouting at the radio, live on Facebook.

But that's what I'm doing – I'm shouting at the radio. I'm in the kitchen every morning, washed and shaved, standing or sitting in front of the radio and

I'm shouting right through the News and on into Seán O'Rourke and Pat Kenny. (I skip Ryan Tubridy; he'd kill me.) And I keep going, right through the Angelus.

—Bong, yourself!

It's a big online hit, that one, the daughter tells me, and we're selling about twenty *Bong, Yourself!* T-shirts a day.

Anyway, I stop about ten minutes into Ronan Collins, after I've hurled abuse at the birthday requests, and I'm given permission to go upstairs for a nap, so I'll be fit and fighting in time for Joe Duffy.

Talk to Joe.

—I will in me hole!

It's not a sudden thing, or a late vocation. I've been shouting at the eejits on the radio all my life. Some men learn how to play the uilleann pipes from their fathers; others are taught how to mend fishing nets, how to keep bees or maim cattle. My da showed me how to shout.

He spent long happy hours instructing me on the correct use of the word 'gobshite'. He didn't know he was doing this; I was just looking at him, and listening. But, nevertheless, that was what he did. I sat in the kitchen with him and learnt all about the different categories of gobshite. There was the 'bloody' gobshite, the 'out and out' gobshite, and the 'complete and utter' gobshite. There was a gobshite for every occasion, a label for every man he shouted at. A younger man just starting out in his career as a gobshite – a newly elected TD, say, or an economist just home from America who wore a cravat instead of a tie – he had 'the makings of a gobshite'. There was still hope for him, but not much. The makings of a gobshite almost always rose through the ranks to become a complete and utter gobshite.

He never shouted at women. Now, there weren't many women on the wireless back then but he wouldn't have shouted at them anyway. In my father's world there was no such thing as a female gobshite.

One thing is vital: he was happy. I spent large chunks of my childhood listening to my da shouting. But it never frightened me – never – and it often made me laugh. My favourite was when he came up from behind his newspaper, like he was climbing out of the pages, and roared.

–Will you listen to that bloody gobshite!

He'd look at me, grin, and go back behind his paper.

He was happy. And – I hate admitting this – so am I. I'm exhausted and I'm spending the waking hours when I'm not shouting sucking throat lozenges. And fair enough, they do the trick. But five packs of Strepsils a day can leave you feeling a bit queasy.

I'm shouting in my sleep too. According to the wife – and I've no reason not to believe her. She always tells the truth and, more often than not, it's brutal.

–Whoever you were dreaming about last night, Charlie, she says. –They were all gobshites.

–Gobshites?

–The bedroom was full of them, she says.

–The room was full of men, so, I tell her.

–In *your* dreams, Charlie, she says. –Not mine.

She smiles. She can see it too: I'm happy. I'm exhausted and jumpy; I haven't seen sunlight since – I can't remember. My throat is killing me and I think I might have scurvy.

But I'm a happy man – I'm a happy father. Because the fact is, I'm not the social influencer: the daughter is. I'm her performing monkey and do exactly what I'm told.

–We're building up the follower numbers, Dad, she says. –Then we'll start campaigning properly, like.

–Campaigning?

–Yeah.

–What's our first target?

–The banks.

I stare at her: do we ever really know our kids?

28

I'm standing out in the back garden with the wife.

Now, in actual fact, we don't have a back garden. We have a hole where there used to be one. We used to have grass. No surprise there, I suppose; it's kind of your basic ingredient, isn't it? But we had a lilac bush that was spectacular for a few weeks in the year, and an apple tree that had real apples hanging off it in the autumn. We had all sorts of flowers. The garden – in its way – was lovely.

Then we got the dogs and they ate it.

Literally.

It was gone in a month. You know those photographs of no man's land, the stretch of muck between the German and British trenches in the First World War? That's what we have now, except there's much more muck.

Don't get me wrong – the dogs are great. They'd never eat anything live – well, human. But we had to make the choice, me and the wife: would we let them eat the house or the garden? So we decided – after some anguish and tears – to sacrifice the garden. It was either that or stand back and let them demolish the contents of the house, including the floors and walls.

It never occurred to us to get rid of the dogs, and that surprises me now. It was a simple choice: house or garden. And, actually, the garden was a goner by the time we had the vote. They'd eaten the tree, the shrubs, the hedge, the rabbit hutch – it was empty; the rabbit had gone up to heaven years before – and most of the shed. They'd left us the walls.

A section of the wall, the one at the very back, we called our memory wall. It was the wife's idea. Everywhere we went, she'd bring home a stone from a beach, say, or a shell or a little tile, and we'd stick them to the wall. It was an idea she got from one of her sisters – Carmel – the sound one. After a while, probably about twenty years, it began to look great. When anyone came to the house and looked out the kitchen window, they'd see the memory wall and go out and have a proper look at it.

Anyway, the dogs didn't eat the wall but they ate all the memories off it. Every stone and shell. The wall, like my mind, is a blank.

You know that phrase, 'You had to laugh'? Well, we did laugh – but we had to work hard at it. The wife had to tickle me and I had to threaten to tickle her.

I should make something clear: we feed the dogs – we feed them well. And we love them. Me, the wife, the kids, the grandkids – all of us love the dogs. And, in fairness, they seem to have big time for us. When they catch me looking out the window at them, all I can see is a sea of wagging tails.

Anyway. Me and the wife are standing in what used to be our back garden. We're out there in the muck and the rain because we're making a video. Well, the daughter's actually making the video. We're just starring in it.

It's going to go up on my *Shouter* Facebook page.

We're Kate and Mick from that ad – you know the one; the couple who've just paid off their mortgage. Most of us, if we manage to clear the mortgage, go out for a drink and maybe something to eat. This pair, though, go on telly ten times a night and thump their chests.

So, anyway. I've grown a handlebar moustache. It's a bit lopsided; there's only one handle. The dogs are charging around us.

–We work well together, says the wife. –We do.

Her American accent is very good.

–Yeah, we do, I agree.

–We have to, says the wife.

The grandson is right behind me and he's just stabbed me in the arse with something sharpish, but I still manage to smile at the wife and she smiles back.

–There are memories in every nook and cranny, she says. –Every mark on the floor.

–They were challenging times, yeah, I say. –A lot of hard work. But we knew we'd come the road together.

–We just knew we'd make it work, says the wife.

Then I turn to the wife and we look back at the house.

–But do you remember the time they threatened to repossess the house? I say. –When I was out of work for a while.

–Bastards, she says.

–Humiliating, I say. –It was terrifying.

–Heartless bastards.

Then the grandson comes out from behind us and holds up his placard: We Back Belief Every Day.

–And … cut, says the daughter.

The grandson sees us crying and he hugs our legs.

29

I've nothing against Bovril. In fact, I'm quite fond of a drop of Bovril. I even put a dab of it behind my ears once – kind of an experiment to see if the dogs would notice.

I woke up in Beaumont A&E.

What happened was this: I'd been down on my hunkers, in among the grandkids, when we'd performed the experiment. The dogs came at me so enthusiastically – before I'd even put the lid back on the jar – that they knocked me backwards and I whacked my head against the side of the fireplace.

When I woke up in Beaumont I was still clutching the Bovril. The wife told me the dogs had attacked the ambulance men when they were trying to get me out of the house on a stretcher.

–The kids thought they were trying to kidnap you, she said.

–The dogs?

–The ambulance men.

–Would you have paid the ransom? I asked her.

Now that I think of it, she never answered.

But, anyway, I went home with my head bandaged, looking a bit like Peter O'Toole in *Lawrence of Arabia*

– I thought – or a sheep's head in butcher's paper – she said. My head was killing me but I was just delighted to get out of the A&E with it still attached to my neck. I once heard about a chap who went in there with a sprained ankle and ended up donating one of his kidneys – a clerical error, they said. But I was safely out, with both kidneys tucked up where they should be, and the wife even got me a milkshake from the Artane McDonald's on the way home. So I was happy enough and I never held it against the dogs – or Bovril.

So, like I said, I've nothing against Bovril. But I don't feel a burning need to keep telling the world that it's my beverage of choice. Because (a) it's not true – it's far from bloody true. And (b) I feel like a gobshite doing it.

But I have to.

I think I do.

It's the daughter's doing again. She tells me I'm a brand ambassador.

We've thousands of people following me on my *Shouter* Facebook page and she says it's time to start cashing in on my popularity.

I stare at her – although it's hard to tell what my face is doing these days. A few weeks back, I thought I was smiling at the young one behind the counter of the Insomnia up the road, but she burst out crying and said she was sorry for my trouble, and she wouldn't let me pay for my cappuccino.

Anyway, she – the daughter – says if I keep mentioning how much I love the product she'll be able to organise a few quid for us from the manufacturers. Now, I'm all for the few quid – I've a special account in the credit union for the grandkids. But, like, there's nothing coursing through my blood telling me to sing out for Bovril.

–Could I not do Hugo Boss? I ask her.

–They've got Gerard Butler, like.

–I wouldn't mind sharing with Gerard, I tell her. –I'm a better actor than he is, anyway.

–Be honest, Dad, she says. –Do you really – really now – know what Hugo Boss is?

I make an educated guess.

–It's either aftershave or underpants, I say. –Am I right?

She doesn't answer. No surprise there, I suppose – she comes from a long line of women who don't bloody answer.

Anyway.

Here I am, sitting at the open kitchen door, looking out at the last of the sun going down behind the back wall. I'm wearing sunglasses and I've a Bovril mug in my hand.

The daughter has her iPad right against my head. She's filming me.

I take a sip.

–Ah, I say – and I *do* have to say it, because I don't mean the 'Ah' – the sigh – if that makes sense.

Or, I do mean the 'Ah' – it's the genuine article, a sigh of genuine satisfaction – because I'm not sipping Bovril. It might say 'Bovril' on the mug but it's full of gin and tonic.

I turn to the camera.

–You can't beat a bit of Bovril at the end of a hard day's shouting, I say. –In fairness.

–We'll have to go again, like, says the daughter.

–Ah Jaysis – why?

–I could see your ice and lemon poking over the side of the mug, she says.

So fair enough. Once more with feeling.

–Dad, she says.

–What, love?

–There's no steam, she says. –There should be steam, like. It's a hot drink.

–No problem, I say. –How's this?

I look at the camera.

–You can't beat an ice-cold Bovril and tonic at the end of a long day doing absolutely fuck-all.

She's laughing.

–Brilliant, she says.

30

I walk past the shop where I bought the suit for my wedding. It's been turned into a Spar.

I go back across the Liffey and come to the bank that turned me and the wife down for our first mortgage. It's a Spar.

The shop where we bought our first good telly – a Spar. The shop where the kids could buy toys for a pound – it's a Spar. The shop where I bought my first Slade record – you've guessed it.

I'm relieved when I get to the top of O'Connell Street and see that the Rotunda is still the Rotunda and not a colossal Spar. Our kids were born in there, and all of the grandkids – except the one who was born on the way there. She's called Summer, because she was born in Summerhill, in the back of a moving taxi.

It seems like nearly all the key buildings of my life – the architectural reminders of the decades I've lived and worked in this city – have become Spars. Why don't they just change the name of the place to Spartown?

The taxi driver – the chap who was driving my daughter-in-law to the Rotunda – was a decent enough skin. He went like the clappers, through a couple of red lights, and up onto the path in Ballybough. The daughter-in-law said she'd name the baby after him if it was a boy, if they made it to the hospital. Then she saw his name on the dashboard. He was African and she couldn't read his name, let alone pronounce it. So he said she could name the baby after the taxi instead. Young Summer did her Junior Cert this year. She has no idea how close she came to being called Toyota.

Anyway, don't get me wrong: I've nothing against Spars.

That's not true. I hate them.

When I was a kid there was a grocer down the road, Mister Baldwin. He wore a brown coat over his suit and he stood outside the shop when he wasn't busy. He always held a brush. He'd pick up the brush, like John Wayne picking up his rifle, before he'd step outside to have a gawk at the world. He lived in the flat above the shop and you'd see his cigarette smoke floating out the window in the evenings, and hear his records – Peggy Lee, Frank Sinatra. He wasn't married and my father once told me that the love of his life was Missis Kelly, who ran the grocer's *up* the road.

–She married the wrong grocer, he said.

–Don't mind him, said my mother.

The only things my mother said more often than 'Don't mind him' were 'Wipe your feet', 'Jesus wept', and 'Ah, God love you.'

Anyway, whether the story was true or not, everyone on the estate thought Mister Baldwin was a lovely man and Missis O'Neill was a weapon.

Except me. I thought Missis O'Neill was the lovely one. The way she leaned on the counter, the way she stared at you like she knew you wanted to rob something, the way she shouted to Mister O'Neill in the back of the shop – *Fergus! Beans!* She was terrifying and the love of my ten-year-old life. Until she ran off with the man who delivered the Rinso. Spotless Tommy, my da called him.

–She'll put spots on that poor gobshite.

–Don't mind him.

Anyway, Mister O'Neill came out from behind the shop and sold it. It became a chipper and he moved to Spain.

I suppose what I'm saying is: the shops had personality. Each one was different. Some were dark, some had a smell that was unique. The people in charge were nice or mad, or ancient or gorgeous, or kind or frightening. The shop was theirs and they all looked a bit like their shop. Mister Baldwin the grocer looked like a big spud – his brown coat was something a potato would wear on his wedding day.

And that's my objection to the Spars: they're all the bloody same. When I walk into a Spar I step out of Dublin, into some boring, half-imagined vision of the future. If I owned a shop I'd want my name over the door, or a name I'd come up with myself, *The House of Savage*, or something like that.

–But it's hard to imagine anyone actually owning a Spar, isn't it? I say to the wife. –An individual human being, like.

I've brought chips home with me and I have my heart set on a chip butty.

–We've no bread, says the wife.

–What?

–We've no bread.

–Ah, Jesus, I say. –Where will I get bread at this hour?

–The Spar, she says.

–Would it still be open?

–Ah, yeah, she says. –It never shuts.

–That's brilliant, I say. –Don't go near the chips. I'll be back in a minute.

31

I haven't gone for a pint in ages.

That's a bit of a fib – it's a lie.

I've been out for a pint a fair few times. But I haven't gone to my local. I've walked in the opposite direction, to a pub that's nearer the house but definitely isn't my local. I've sat there on my own – no one to talk to, no one I want to talk to. If the Canadian geese migrate to Dublin every winter, then all of Dublin's gobshites migrate to this place every night. It's like a gobshite zoo – it has every variety. And it leaves me wondering: am I a gobshite too?

Probably.

I'm miserable most of the time; it seems to be my natural state. But there's a big difference between being happily miserable and being just miserable. And sitting in that place on my own, nursing a sloppy pint that was pulled by a barman who's more interested in his beard than in his profession – well, I'm just miserable. I've even started wearing my reading glasses on my head, so I can read my phone while I'm there. That's how fuckin' miserable I am.

The glasses on the head – the wife doesn't like the look.

–When did your dandruff start reading, Charlie? she says.

I don't even defend myself and my dandruff – or the absence of it.

I miss my buddy, the Secret Woman. The time has come to name him. His name is Martin and I miss him.

We didn't have a row, exactly – although that's what I told the wife. Martin came with me when I was going to meet Eileen Pidgeon in Greystones a few months back. Eileen was my first real girlfriend. We went with each other for two days and a bit; that's a lifelong commitment when you're sixteen and you measure your life in hours. I met her again on Facebook. I'll be honest: I went out of my way to meet her on Facebook.

I'm definitely a gobshite.

So anyway, we were in a café in Greystones, myself, Eileen and Martin. I went to the jacks and the other pair availed of the opportunity to get off with each other. They were holding hands – or they had been, if that makes sense – when I got back. And – I'll be honest again – I was happy enough to have the excuse to storm out and leg it home.

But it was humiliating. Martin told me just after Christmas that he identified as a woman, so I'd never have expected him to do the dirty on me. And he'd also assured me, hand on heart, that he wasn't a lesbian. I know, we're living in an age of what I think the daughter calls gender fluidity, and I'm grand with it – or I'm trying to be. But Martin with Eileen – that was just having his cake and eating it.

So, sitting on the Dart out of Greystones, I was relieved but hurt. And I haven't seen Martin since. I've been tempted to text him or just wander up to the local. But I'm afraid of what I might find there: Eileen Pidgeon with her arse parked on the stool where my arse should be.

I don't want to meet Eileen.

Listen: I'm a happily married man – although I'm not sure what 'happily married' actually means. We've been together more than forty years and I can't say I've been deliriously happy all that time. But I'm betting I've been happier because I've been sharing the years – the house, the kids, the grandkids, the bed, the crisps, the books, the hoodies, the laughs and the grief – with her. She walks into the room and I sit up. She kisses me like she means it. She laughs at my jokes, especially the intentional ones. And she makes me laugh.

I love her. Simple as that. And as complicated.

So I don't want to see Eileen Pidgeon.

But I do want to see Martin. A man without friends isn't really a man. I've no idea what that means – but it feels true.

So I send him a text. The usual text – or what used to be the usual one. *Pint?* I'm not waiting long; he's back in twenty seconds. *Yep.*

So far, so good.

I tell the wife.

–I'm going for a pint with Martin.

–I'm glad, she says.

–Yeah, I say. –I texted him.

–Good, she says.

She hugs me.

–You even shaved for the occasion, she says.

–I did.

–And you're wearing your Old Spice, she says.

–I am.

She pats my chest.

–And your Jamie Redknapp shirt.

–Yep.

–And you ironed it and all.

–Yep.

–To meet Martin.

–Well, I say. –Like – it feels a bit special.

–I know, she says, and she kisses me.

I really, really – true as God – do not want to meet Eileen Pidgeon.

32

I push the pub door open.

No, that's a mistake. I pull it open. But the point is: I feel like I'm pushing it. I'm a cowboy – a desperado – pushing the swinging saloon doors open with both hands and striding right in. Although I'm guessing that striding successfully would be tricky enough after four days on a horse.

Anyway, I walk into the local.

And he's there, ahead of me. My pal, Martin – the Secret Woman – is sitting exactly where I wanted to see him, one stool to the left of the Guinness tap.

And he's alone. He has his phone out, texting – I think. The stool beside him – my stool – is empty. I walk right up and park myself.

–Alright?

–Pint?

–Go on ahead.

He lifts a finger to Raymond the barman, who goes to the Guinness tap and picks up an empty glass on his way. He's only three feet away but he leaves us alone. I look around. All is as it should be. Familiar heads, and not too many of them. Tennis on the telly – no one watching it.

Martin fires off a text and puts the phone in his pocket. He looks at me.

One thing: Martin doesn't do smiling. And it's not because he's a bit older and has become, like most men our age, facially confusing. And he didn't stop smiling when his wife died. He's never been a smiler. He only has the one face, a bit like Buster Keaton. You have to know him well to know when he's happy or amused. It's in the shoulders; he sits up or stands straighter – becomes a taller man.

Anyway, he looks at me.

–I hate this time of the year, he says.

And that gets us on our way. He means the lack of football. We're miserable in the summer and have always enjoyed being miserable together. We fill the hungry months with transfer rumours, the Dubs, the holidays, the state of the world and, occasionally, the state of ourselves.

We don't talk about Greystones or Eileen Pidgeon. We don't even mention Greystones or Eileen Pidgeon.

We practise the pronunciation of the players our teams – I'm Man United; he, God love him, is Chelsea – might be buying during the summer.

–Bakayoko.

–Is it not Bakayoko?

–No, I think it's Bakayoko.

–Is he French or what?

–He's French.

–And he's good?

–Brilliant.

–You've seen him play?

–No. But he's brilliant.

For a while we say nothing at all. And that's grand too; we're men who are happy in our silence. He picks up his pint. I pick up mine.

–Good pint tonight, he says.

–Yeah, I answer.

The pint is good – the same – every night. But we like to remind ourselves that we're veterans of the Bad Pint Wars. We grew up with stories of bad pints, bad pubs, vomiting, hospitalisations, pints so dreadful the drinkers were hallucinating for weeks after, waking up in Korea after going to the jacks; tales of evil landlords emptying slop trays into Guinness kegs, when every pint was a potential near-death experience. It was our Vietnam.

I put my pint back down.

–Adequate.

He puts his down.

–Yep.

I know she's there before I see her. Eileen Pidgeon has just sashayed into the saloon – sorry, pub. It's a fact before I know it. Because of Martin's face.

He smiles.

For the first time in the decades I've known him, his face – well, it transforms. Buster Keaton becomes Cary Grant – or Cary Grant's da. I'm sitting beside a stranger. And a handsome stranger – the bastard.

I turn, and Eileen is already sitting on the stool beside me. She's not actually on it but she's getting there; she's negotiating it, hoisting herself like a determined toddler.

That's not fair.

Eileen had a hip replacement a few years back – I read that on her Facebook page – and, taking that into consideration, she's up on the stool like Nadia Comaneci on the beam. If I had a card and a marker, I'd give her a 9.7.

I'm stuck between them – sandwiched between them.

I look at him. I look at her. I look at him.

–Charlie, she says.

I look at her.

–How are you, pet?

–Grand, I say.

I look away.

Pet?

I can't cope with this. One minute I'm having a quiet pint with my best friend, the next I'm in the Rover's Return, in a scene from *Coronation Street*, one of those dramatic ones just before the ads, when someone's going to get thumped. That's what it feels like. No one's going to hit me but I still feel like I've just woken up in the middle of a shite drama. I half-expect the *Corrie* music.

But I look at Martin. I mightn't be happy but – Christ now – he is.

33

There are things that we give up on as we get older, and things that give up on us. Eyesight, hair, self-respect; they all walk out the door. Memory strolls out too, and it leaves the door wide open.

But it's not all bad. Take blushing, for example. I used to be a shocking blusher, the redner king of the Northside. I couldn't lie with any sort of aplomb; I was hopeless. I could come up with a good porky, no bother – there was nothing wrong with my imagination. But I couldn't deliver it. My cheeks, my whole face, my neck would be scarlet before I'd finished talking, before I'd even started. I was my own lie detector. My ears would actually hurt, they got so hot.

There's one lie I remember particularly well. I was seventeen and my mother had just smelled bottled Guinness off my breath.

–I was just tasting it for Kevo's granda, I told her.
–His taste buds are gone so he asked me to check it for him.

It was a good lie, I thought. I'd have believed it, myself. At least I'd have given it serious consideration, before pronouncing sentence and booking the executioner.

But my mother was looking at me turning into Poolbeg Lighthouse in a Thin Lizzy T-shirt and elephant flares. I was announcing the lie as I was making it up.

So I gave up telling fibs; there was no point. I composed some good ones for my brothers and sisters.

–Here, Charlie. I'll be staying out all night, so I need two good lies and a verifiable alibi.

It was a good little earner for the last few years of school – fifty pence a porky. But, really, I yearned to tell my own lies. But I couldn't. I blushed well into my thirties.

I remember when it stopped. I told the wife her hair was lovely and she believed me. The hair was a disaster; she looked like your man from Kajagoogoo.

–What d'you think? she asked.

She was terrified.

–It's lovely, I said.

The terror dropped off her face. And my own face – I could feel it; it wasn't hot. My blushing days were over and I could lie with impunity.

–It accentuates your cheekbones, I told her.

I had no idea what that meant but she was all over me for days.

I never expected to blush again. And I didn't – until now.

Eileen Pidgeon has just sat on the stool beside me. My pal, Martin, is on the other side. One minute I was chatting about the football, the next I'm the spare prick at the wedding.

And my face goes on fire. It's not just my imagination. I can see myself in the mirror behind the bar. I'm the same colour as the Man United jersey – and not their away jersey. I start scratching my neck. There are fire ants starting to nest right under my chin; they're

126

digging in and stinging like bejaysis – that's what it feels like.

But the lovebirds don't seem to notice. They're chatting over my head.

–Did you get anything interesting in town?

–Ah no, not really – just the usual, you know.

–Grand.

Is it possible to be mortified and bored at the same time?

–I got us a couple of lasagnes from Marks and Sparks, she tells him.

–Brilliant.

–And strawberries.

–Ah, massive, he says. –I love a good strawberry.

A minute ago we were analysing some of the world's best football talent. Now he's writing poetry about soft fruit.

The man is clearly in love.

It's unbearable. I'm going to have to leave. I'm in the way. There won't be enough lasagne for three. Anyway, I've already had lasagne today and I made it myself – none of your shop-bought shite.

I feel homeless – even though I'll be going home.

–Are you having a drink, love? he asks her.

Love?

–Ah, no, she says. –I just came in to say hello to Charlie.

She kisses me on the cheek – I'm burning again – and slides down off the stool. Then she gathers up her bags.

I've hardly looked at her. But I look at her now. I think I smile. She definitely does.

–See you later, pet, she says to Martin.

–Yeah, seeyeh.

I watch her leave, and turn to him.

–Yis are living together?

–Tuesdays and Thursdays, he says.

–It's Wednesday, I tell him.

–I know, he says. –But I didn't have the heart to tell her.

He smiles.

–Thanks for introducing us, by the way.

It only occurs to me now: that's what I actually did. And, I'm not sure why, but it makes me happy – kind of.

–Does she know you identify as a woman? I ask him.

He stares at me now.

–I told her, yeah.

–And she's fine with it?

–Yeah, he says. –I think it's why she couldn't wait till Thursday.

34

The holidays used to be easier. They were nearly always disastrous; I'm not denying that. But they were more straightforward. You went into Joe Walsh or Budget Travel just after Christmas and got their brochures. You went home and sat with the wife until she decided where you were going. Then you went back in the next day, got into the queue and booked it.

Done.

You'd seen a photograph of the outside of the apartment in the brochure. You knew it would be 'a two-minute walk' from the beach and five minutes on the bus from the 'old' town. Disappointment was inevitable – 'That was the longest two minutes of my life; I've worn a hole in my fuckin' espadrilles' – but that was part of the package. You could sit around the pool, if there actually was a pool, and give out.

We're good at that, the Irish, having a laugh at our collective bad luck. We never really minded when we discovered that the apartment was miles from the beach, or that it wasn't even in Spain. We'd burst our shites laughing as it dawned on us that the locals weren't speaking Spanish. As long as we got badly scorched and at least one of the kids had to be rushed to the local hospital, we were happy enough. Just as long as we had a good story to bring home with us.

–I was sitting on the jacks all of the second week.

–That's gas.

–Ah now – it was a bit more than gas.

These days, though, booking a holiday is as tricky as open-heart surgery. I wouldn't dream of performing surgery on myself or anyone else. I'm not a surgeon or a plumber or a chef, but I'm expected to be my own travel agent. It's terrifying. One mistake and you're broke or lost.

Last year we – myself and the wife, the daughter and her little lad – went to the Algarve. It's a nice enough spot but it took us five days to get there.

The wife booked the apartment and that was straight-forward enough. We went on an online tour of it – and there it all was, the kitchen, bedrooms, sitting room with a bowl of fruit, a little balcony with a chair.

–That'll do us, I said.

I was standing beside her, looking at the laptop.

–I don't know, she said. –It won't let us see the view from the balcony.

–More balconies is my bet, I said. –With loads of Paddies waving back at us.

The problems were planted when she booked the flights. It's a rule that will never make any sense to me: the more connecting flights, the cheaper the journey. We'd left it late, so a direct flight to Faro was going to cost us an arm and a good bit of a leg. But we could get there for €37 each if we went via Tirana, Prague and Samarkand.

–Four countries for the price of one, I said. –Brilliant.

She laughed and booked us.

I'll say just one thing: the full Irish breakfast in Tirana Airport isn't the best. The Albanians are a proud and hospitable people but they haven't a clue what to do with a rasher.

We lost the grandson in Prague Airport and found him just as he was boarding a flight to Chile.

But anyway, we had four terrific days in Portugal before we had to head home.

–Never again, said the wife.

She actually got the words tattooed on her shoulder – in Tirana Airport, during the seventeen-hour stopover.

So this year we decided to go nowhere. We told the family we were doing the Camino, from Sarria to Santiago de Compostela. But we're hiding in the house. I had to sneak out last night to get milk but, other than that, we've been at home, behind closed curtains, for the last two weeks.

And it's been brilliant. We've been going through all those programmes we can't watch when the grandson's in the house. We're well into the second series of *The Affair*. It's absolutely filthy.

–Beats the Camino, says the wife.

And I'm with her.

We've got through all of *Game of Thrones* and I've started calling her Cersei.

She stares at me.

–Everyone who isn't us is our enemy, she says, and takes a bite of the beef and bacon pizza I'm holding out for her.

Her phone rings.

It's the daughter, checking on us.

–Hi, love, says the wife. –No, no, it's not too hot today. It's just nice.

I get her iPad and turn on the thing we found on YouTube, a gang of nuns saying the Hail Mary in Spanish.

–I can't hear you, love, says the wife. –I'll phone you back when the nuns have passed.

She throws the phone on the couch.

We look at each other and howl.

35

The world's in a desperate state. There's a nut in charge of North Korea and an even bigger nitwit in charge of America. Nuclear war seems inevitable, or death by Brexit. The monotony of that thing – Jesus. Soon, we'll all just lie down where we are and die of boredom. But the news – terrorist attacks, famines, disasters, intolerance – it's relentlessly dreadful. Even the good murder stories have become too gruesome for me. Our parents left the world in reasonably good shape but I've a horrible feeling we'll be leaving it in rag order.

And I'm in rag order, myself. I'm halfway down the stairs in the morning before I'm convinced that I'm awake, that I'm actually alive. There's an ache in my wrist when I pick up the kettle. I stare at the tap before I remember why I'm standing in front of it with the same bloody kettle. I've a piece of paper sellotaped to the bathroom mirror: 'Your name is Charlie.' I can remember the rest myself but I need the nudge – every morning and sometimes later – before I go out for a pint. Knowing your own name might not be essential when you're heading out the door to your local but, in my experience, it makes for a much more relaxing evening. I sometimes wish I was called Guinness. Then I'd only have to remember the one vital name.

Anyway. The world's in bits and so am I. But I don't care. The football's back and there's a spring in my limp.

There's nothing like the optimism of the football fan in August. He – or she – skips through the drudgery of daily life as if it's a fairy tale created just for him by Disney. The happy ending is only ninety minutes away – with time added on. History has been wiped. Last season's disasters – the last decade's disasters – have been forgotten. This is the year.

Listen to any Leeds United fan in early August – if you can stomach it.

–This is *the* year, he'll tell you.

He's been saying that, once a year, since 2004 when they were relegated, and I'm betting his great-grandad was saying it in 1924.

'This is the year.' The poor sap will be suicidal by the start of September but he'll be back again next August, all set for a fresh start in the giddy delights of League One – or the Third Division, as it should be called. 'I'm telling you, bud – this is the year.'

August is the month that gets me through the other eleven. I could do a Rip Van Winkle, drop off to sleep for years, and wake up in August, knowing immediately that the football was back. I'd feel it in the bones, or on my skin, before I'd know what had happened to me. The angle of the sun or something – I'd know that *Match of the Day* was back on the telly before I'd realise that, somehow, I was 127 and that the little oul' lad staring down at me was my grandson. I'd ask him where everyone else was and how Manchester United were doing – but not necessarily in that order.

On Saturday nights, August to May, my father shifted a bit in his chair and let me and my brothers get in beside him. He'd have been out for his few pints and he always stopped at the chipper on his way home – two singles to be divided between the lot of us. When I hear the *Match of the Day* music, I smell salt and vinegar – and my father.

And I hear him.

–The reception's not too bad, lads. We might actually see the match tonight.

He taught us how to love.

–Ah, Jesus, lads – Georgie Best. Look at what he just did.

And he taught us how to hate.

–Your man, Billy Bremner there, lads. He's an evil little bollix.

–Don't listen to him, said my mother.

But we listened to every word. We had our da to ourselves on the big chair that was our whole world. He was teaching us how to cheer and groan, to shout, to laugh together and suffer together in silence.

A well taken goal makes me feel exactly like I felt way more than fifty years ago, when I was squashed in beside my father. A goal by that young lad, Marcus Rashford, or our new lad, Lukaku – and the texts will start arriving from the brothers. *Jaysis! 4 F SAKE! How did he manage that?!!!*

–Ah, Jesus, referee! my father shouted. –Where's your white stick? What is he, Charlie?

–A stupid bloody bastard, Da.

–Good man.

–Don't listen to him, said my mother.

I always knew when my father was smiling; I didn't have to see him.

–What do you do if a woman smiles at you, Charlie?

–Run like the clappers, Da.

–Good man.

36

The wife is furious.

–I'm telling you now, she says.

She repeats these words every time she opens a press, looks in, and slams it shut. We're in the kitchen, by the way.

–I'm telling you now.

She's staring into the cutlery drawer. I can hear the teaspoons whimpering. The drawer's a bit bockety, so she can't slam it shut.

–I'm telling you now, she says, and she looks at me. –Whoever took it will be met with fire and fury like the world has never seen.

Someone's after robbing her Flake.

–I'll get you another one, I say.

–I don't want another one.

–It's no bother, I say. –I'll be back in five minutes.

–No!

She takes a breath, holds it – lets it go.

–No, she says. –No. Thanks.

I'm being a bit brave here.

–It's only a Flake, love, I say.

She looks at me.

–I know, she says.

Then she gives the cutlery drawer an almighty kick.

She sits down. I think she's hurt her foot – and her hip. But I know: she'll wait a while before she'll admit it.

–One little thing, she says. –A treat for myself.

–I know.

–And it's gone.

–I know, I say. –It's not fair.

She's looking down at her foot.

–Is your foot sore, love?

–No!

–Grand.

–Yes! It's very bloody sore!

–Oh, I say. –Right.

I'd get down on the floor and rub the foot for her but it would seem a bit biblical or something – something the Pope would do. And I've a feeling she'd kick me. So, I stay put.

But it's terrible, seeing her upset.

I see an upset man and I'll know why he's upset, immediately. His team has lost, his dog has died, he's just seen the state of himself in the jacks mirror. I can read all men – except myself.

I see an upset woman – I'm mystified. I haven't a clue. But I try my best.

–Is it the change, love? I ask her.

–What?

I'm already regretting this.

–Well, like, I say. –Is it the change?

–Jesus, Charlie, she says. –I'm sixty!

She laughs but it isn't a happy sound – at all.

–Why didn't you ask me that – Jesus – years ago? she asks.

–There's only the one then, is there?

–One what, exactly?

–Change.

She stares at me.

–Just the one, so, I say. –That's handy enough, isn't it?

This time her laugh actually sounds like laughter – *her* laughter. It's my favourite thing about her. The first time I saw her I thought she was lovely. Then she laughed and – Christ – I felt like I'd been thumped in the chest by an angel.

Anyway, she's laughing now because of something I said, and that makes me the happiest man in the kitchen. I'm alive – I'm the same man I was forty years ago, making the same woman laugh.

But she's not happy – I can tell. She's going to say something. There's a little crease just above her right eyebrow that shifts slightly when she's getting ready to talk. It's been joined by a few more creases since the first time I noticed it, but I still know the one to look for.

–I just feel – I don't know, she says now. –A bit hard done by.

I know how she feels. But I don't say that. I learnt that lesson years ago.

Thirty-seven years ago.

–Oh Christ, I'm in agony! she screamed.

–Same here, I told her.

She grabbed my arm and squeezed. We were in the Rotunda and she gave birth to our eldest ten minutes later. If you look carefully, you can still see the bruises on my arm.

Anyway.

–And I'm right to feel hard done by, she says now.

–You are, I agree.

139

–I'm not a selfish woman, Charlie, she says.

–No.

–Sure I'm not?

–No, I say. –You're – listen. You're the least selfish person I know.

She smiles.

–I hid that bloody Flake so I could have it while we were watching *Riviera,* she says.

Riviera's a load of shite but I keep the review to myself.

–It's silly, I know, she says. –But – . Some louser's after stealing it and it's not bloody fair.

The house was full earlier, countless kids and grandkids. She fed them all. She was the perfect granny, the perfect mother. I'd nearly cried, looking at her with the grandkids.

–It's crap, I tell her.

I take her hands and lift her from the chair. I hug her and kiss the side of her face.

–I love you, I tell her.

She slides her hand into the back pocket of my jeans and squeezes my arse – or, where my arse used to be. And she feels something in the pocket.

–What's this? she says, and she takes it out.

Oh, shite.

It's the Flake wrapper.

37

I'm in the jacks.

Not at home – in the local. Anyway, I'm in there. And I'm – I'll use the formal expression – I'm urinating. Now, normally I wouldn't be telling you this and you, I'm sure, would be happier if I wasn't. But there's a chap standing beside me and he isn't – urinating, that is. He's making a film.

I'm just standing there, minding my own business. Staring at the wall. And humming. *Knowing me, knowing you – ahaaaaaaa—!* Counting the tiles. When I'm aware that there's someone beside me. I don't look but I'm assuming it's a man. You get the odd girl straying into the Gents but she usually cops on quickly and she never, ever strolls up to the urinal unbuttoning her fly.

Anyway, like I said, I'm aware of someone beside me. Nothing unusual there – there's room for three good-sized men, as long as they're not doing the hokey-cokey.

But this chap is talking – and not to me.

In the world of the urinal silence is golden. I know, there are men who are incapable of silence. If they're not talking, they're groaning. The unbuckling of the belt, and a groan. The unbuttoning/unzipping of the fly – a groan. The search for the little brother – groan. The

141

meeting of the waters – groan. It's not age-related. If he's groaning when he's ten, he'll be groaning when he's ninety. And there are men who think they're commentating on *Match of the Day*. 'Here we go – yes – !' I know a chap who comes into the jacks humming the theme music from *The Dam Busters*, getting louder as he gets nearer to the urinal. He's been doing this two or three times – and, as he gets older, five, six, seven times a night – every night, since the film came out in 1955.

So, silence is rare in the pub jacks but it shouldn't be like Paris between the wars; philosophy and bullshit should be left outside beside your pint. When your fly's shut, you can open your mouth. That's my philosophy.

But, anyway, this chap beside me is different. He's not groaning and he isn't trying to get me to chat about the rain or Newcastle United. I look to my right, very discreetly, and see his phone. He's holding it up to his face with one hand. And he's yapping away.

I can tell: he's not talking to anyone in particular – he's not skyping his kids in Canada. He's only about thirty, and he has the hair all the young lads have, gelled so hard it might be made of wood.

–So, yeah, he says. –Now I'm in the toilet of a – like – genuine Dublin pub!

And – I swear to God – he points the phone down at the channel.

I jump back. Have you ever zipped up your fly and jumped back at the same time? It's not easy – it should be an Olympic event. But I manage it without cracking my head against the hand dryer. A Dyson, by the way.

Anyway. Outrage isn't something I feel very often. Or, if I do, I'm usually enjoying it – if that makes sense. There's nothing like a bit of well-managed outrage to get the blood going.

But this – here in the pub jacks – is genuinely outrageous. It's an invasion of – well, everything.

–What are you at?! I yell at your man.

–What? he says.

He looks genuinely baffled. And that's the problem – that's the wall between this young lad, about thirty, and me, more than twice his age. He sees nothing wrong in filming himself – and me – going to the jacks in a pub toilet and I don't have the words to even start telling him that it's about as wrong as it gets. I'd do a better job trying to explain the rules of hurling in Japanese. He's grown up filming everything, and being sent everything. If I ask him to, he'll flick through his phone and show me the birth of his nephew, the death of his granny, the vomit he woke up beside at the Electric Picnic, his girlfriend, his boyfriend, his breakfast, his Holy Communion – everything.

I see it at home, my kids trotting after their kids with their cameras. And now the grandkids are toddling after the parents with *their* cameras.

–G'anda, 'ook!

It's the daughter's little lad and he's holding up her iPad; there's something I have to see.

–What's this? I ask him.

–Poo!

He's right. I'm looking at a photo of his first independent poo.

–Good man, I say. –Did you do that all by yourself?

–Yes!

I should be appalled but I pick him up and hug him.

I look now at the young lad in the jacks.

–I'm not an Equity member, son, I tell him. –And neither is my langer.

I walk out without using the Dyson.

143

38

The wife's been warning me all week.

–Don't say anything, Charlie. Just don't say anything. That's all I ask.

Her cousin is coming to the house, with her wife.

–Her wife?

–I told you about her, she says. –Olive. She used to stay with us for the summer holidays. She'd get the train and ferry from London, by herself. I told you, Charlie. Remember? She's gay. She had to get on the train and ferry all by herself.

I do remember. She's told me before, about her cousin from England who came to Dublin to stay with her auntie and uncle and her cousins for July and August, because her father was dead and her mother worked in a car factory and followed her over for the last two weeks of August, and they'd all go to Skerries until the cousin – Olive – and her mother went back to England, back to work and school.

So, I know the story and I know the cousin is gay. But the way the wife is telling the story now, there seems to be a connection I've missed before.

–Are you saying she's gay cos she went on the ferry? I ask her.

144

She stares at me.

–Cos I've been on the Holyhead boat myself a few times and it's never had that effect on me.

Normally, she'd laugh. Well, maybe not laugh. She might just smile, or lift one side of her mouth – I like that one – or whack my shoulder and call me an eejit. But she walks away.

She's nervous.

And that annoys me. It's like she's blaming me for something that hasn't happened yet – that isn't ever going to happen. I'll open my mouth, put my foot in it, insult the woman. But I know: I won't. Her cousin is gay and married to another woman, and I couldn't care less.

I took the word 'normal' out of my vocabulary years ago and put it up on top of the fridge, along with the chipped cups, the flask with the missing lid, the iodine tablets the Government sent out to protect us from nuclear fallout and every other useless thing that we never get around to throwing out. I know: there's no such thing as normal – or, what we used to be told was normal – and I'm happy enough with that.

Mammy, daddy, four, five, six or seven kids and a dog. That was normal when I was a kid. That was our house, actually. That was everybody's house – unless you started looking. Then you found the daddy who worked somewhere far away and never came home, or the mammy who wasn't dead but wasn't there. Or the house with no kids. Or the house with the grown-up son who never left and never had a girlfriend. *He's a bit light on his feet.* Or the house that had two women living in it – friends. That was my road before you got to the corner. Normal has always been complicated but we couldn't say that out loud until a few years ago

– about the same time the Government sent out those iodine tablets.

So, the wife warning me to behave myself – it's not fair.

My best friend, Martin, identifies as a woman and he's having some kind of elderly torrid affair with the woman I kissed when I was sixteen, and she – Eileen Pidgeon – seems to be all over him because he'd rather be a woman but he's a man. And he tells me all about it while we both drink Guinness, which has been the exact same since 1759. That's my normal.

I'm just on my way to have it out with the wife when she walks back into the kitchen.

–There's another thing, she says. –Olive's wife is transgender.

–Ah, Jesus, I say. –I'll need a geometry set and a dictionary to sort this one out.

This time she smiles, or tries to. But she still looks a bit nervous – a bit sad.

–We weren't really nice to her, she says.

–What?

–Olive, she says. –We weren't nice to her. When we were kids, like. We gave her a terrible time.

–Why?

–Well, she says.

She holds the back of one of the chairs with both hands. The table is set, ready for dinner.

–We resented her, for a start, she says. –All the fuss, you know. Olive this, Olive that. And she was English – even though she did all the Irish dancing and that. But – we. No—. *I* sensed she was different, you know. A bit different – even then. And I – I bullied her. That's it. I bullied her.

–We've come a long way, love.

She eventually nods.

The doorbell goes.

–That'll be them.

I go across to the fridge, take down the iodine tablets and throw them on the table.

–Just in case, I say.

39

I see her the first time when I'm out walking some of the dogs.

The fact is, the dogs walk me. I've both hands full of leads, both arms pulled out of their sockets; I'm trying to hang on to four nappy bags full of dog poo and stay upright at the same time.

The dogs love going for their walk but they wait till we're nearly home before they get really excited. They scratch and pull at the ground to make the house come closer to them. You'd swear they were emigrants coming home for Christmas.

–They miss their mammy, I tell the wife.

–Don't we all, she says.

She pretends she doesn't care about the dogs but I've seen the look on her face, the soft, dreamy expression, when she's gazing out the kitchen window at them.

–They're great, aren't they? I say.

–What?

–The dogs.

She takes her glasses from the top of her hair and puts them on her nose. She looks out the window again.

–Oh, yeah, she says. –There they are.

Anyway, I'm nearly home, just across the road from the house, when I see the woman in the car. It's actually the kids I see first, a gang of them in the back behind her, looking out at the dogs and waving and knocking at the side window. I'm in a hurry – well, the dogs are in a hurry – so I make a face at the kids and keep going, across the road, under a bin lorry, and up to the house.

I'm on my way out again a few hours later. Every couple of weeks the wife looks at me.

–Oul' lad's hair, Charlie, she says.

She's telling me to go to the barber, so that's where I'm off to. I've never told her she has oul' one's hair. But that's probably because she never does – not even first thing in the morning when even children can look a bit ancient, especially if it's a schoolday.

Anyway, I'm shutting the front door and I see that the car is still there, across the road – and the woman and the kids. There's something – I don't know. I go over and tap on her window.

She rolls it down.

–Are you alright? I ask her.

She looks a bit nervous – like she's been caught or something. I regret tapping on the glass now. I don't want to make her feel bad. I should have left her alone.

She nods.

–I'm grand, she says. –Thanks.

One of the kids – I think there's four of them in there – waves out at me. I wave back.

–Okay, I say.

I step away from the car and continue on my way.

I usually enjoy going to the barber. I like the wait and the chat. The barber's a Turkish lad but he sounds like he's been getting elocution lessons from Conor McGregor. And he never shuts up. I think he supports every football team in the world – he loves everything. But this time, walking home, I can't even remember if I actually got my hair cut.

I'm thinking about the car and the woman and I'm hoping she won't be there when I turn the corner.

But she is.

The car's there and she's still in it with the kids. I cross the road before I get to it and go on to our front door. I've the key in my hand – and I stop.

She sees me this time, before I tap her window.

–Is the car broken, love?

She shakes her head.

–No.

She smiles.

–Thanks, she says. –I'm just waiting on Lizzie.

Lizzie and Keith live in the house behind me. They moved in a few years back. They're half my age and I love watching their kids playing football in the front garden.

I look back at the house.

–Is she in there?

–Yeah, says the woman. –She's put a wash into her dryer for me. I'll be gone when it's done.

The penny drops, like I knew it would. She has nowhere to go; she's homeless. Her and her kids. I can see now: she's been watching me cop on.

–The kids are quiet enough, I say.

–They're getting used to it, she says.

I don't ask her what 'it' means; I know what 'it' means.

–D'you want a cup of tea? I ask her.

–No, she says. –No, thanks.

I want to ask her if she has somewhere to go tonight. But I don't – I can't. I don't. I'm afraid she'll say No. And what will I do then?

150

–You sure about the tea? I ask.

–No, she says. –Yeah. Thanks. I'll be heading off soon.

–Okay.

I go home. I make myself busy. For an hour, two hours.

It's dark. I go to our bedroom window.

The car is still out there.

40

What gobshite decided that serving tea in a glass was a good idea? I'm not sure if there are any references to tea in the Bible but I'm betting that Jesus and the lads had theirs in mugs. And his holy mother – with a name like Mary she definitely drank hers from a cup and she went down to the Irish shop in Nazareth for the milk. And a packet of Tayto for Joseph – salt and vinegar.

Anyway.

I'm not mad about tea; I rarely touch it. When I was a kid, about fifteen, I was in Dandy Mulcahy's house. We were playing records, chatting about the local young ones, and deciding whether we'd open one of his da's bottles of Smithwick's.

I was very keen. It wasn't my house; it wasn't my da.

–Go on, Dandy.

–No.

–Go on, I said. –He'll never miss it. I'll smuggle the empty out.

–Okay.

Then his ma came in and asked us if we wanted a cup of tea. And Dandy changed. My best friend turned into an oul' lad right in front of my eyes. The mere mention of tea and he forgot all about the mysteries of bottled Smithwick's and the much more promising mysteries of Eileen Pidgeon.

He sat up and clapped his hands.

–Tea! he said. –Rapid!

He instantly became a lad I didn't know. His face, his expression, changed completely. One minute, he was my blood brother and we were all set for a life of beer and women. The next, he looked like someone from the audience of the *Late Late Show* – you know the ones I mean – and he was baying for tea and a Goldgrain.

Bloody tea – I haven't trusted it since.

But I'm not giving out about tea. It's the clown who decided to serve it up in a glass – that's my gripe.

Myself and the daughter are in town with her little lad. She has that look in her eye: she's going to make me try on a metrosexual pair of trousers. So I head her off at the pass and suggest that we go for a coffee and maybe a muffin, if her conscience, which I'm betting wears Lycra, will let her.

–You're hilarious, Dad, she says. –I don't think.

But anyway, we go into this café place that she's found on her phone. It's a bit intimidating but I tell her I want a black coffee and she translates that for the tall lad with the beard behind the counter. He nods, raises his eyes to heaven, and starts knocking the bejaysis out of his machine.

The daughter's ordered black tea – it's good for something or other – and she gets it in a tall glass. And the little lad is having a Coke. She only lets him have one Coke a month. The poor kid is only three and doesn't even know what a month is, so he's like a starving dog in front of a sirloin. I have to hold him by the collar and loosen my grip when he's calm enough for another sip.

But, anyway, we get chatting, me and the daughter, and I must have let go of the little lad's collar. Because the next thing I know, he's screaming and clutching his throat.

–What's wrong?!

I've had two heart attacks so far, and I think I'm after biting half an inch off my tongue.

He looks fine; there's no blood.

He's after mixing up the tea and the Coke, that's all, because they're both in similar glasses. And he's furious.

–T'aum-a-tise!

–What did he say? I ask the daughter.

I can usually understand him but this is a new one.

–He's traumatised, she tells me.

–Did he say that?

And he says it again.

–T'aum–a–tise, G'anda!

His eyes have gone into the back of his head and I'm half-expecting his head to start spinning. I pick him up and put him on my knee. It usually works, and it does now, once we let him clutch his glass – the one with the bloody Coke in it. He holds it on *his* knee.

–Where did he learn that? I ask the daughter.

But I know already – the radio, the telly, everywhere. I was traumatised, myself, this morning when there was no honey for my porridge. He must have heard me but I was only joking – kind of.

–Listen, I tell him now. –If you want to know if you're really traumatised, just put 'Joe' at the end of the sentence. Are you with me?

He's full of sugar and taking in every word.

154

–Say after me, I tell him. –'I was traumatised, Joe.'

–T'aum–a–tise, Doe!

–That's the 'Joe' Test, I tell him. –If there's a 'Joe' at the end of it, it's not really trauma.

–T'aum–a–tise, Doe!

And he knocks back his Coke.

41

We've gone mad for the box sets, me and the wife. I'm beginning to really understand what the word 'addiction' means. If I don't see Helen from *The Affair* at least once a day I come out in a rash; red blotches start crawling across my neck. It's not that I fancy her; I don't. Well, that's a lie. But I worry about her. It's nearly like watching football; I want to shout at the telly. *You could do a lot better than him, love!*

So anyway, I wake up in a sweat at three in the morning, worried sick about Helen. I know I won't get back to sleep, so I slither downstairs, to have a sneaky look at the next episode, to see how Helen is getting on – and I find the wife there ahead of me, gazing at Don Draper in *Mad Men*, Season 7.

We'd watched the other six seasons in a day and a half. That's seventy-eight episodes in thirty-six hours, which is actually impossible – but we still managed it. We work well as a team, me and the wife. We kept each other awake and when one of us went out to the kitchen or the jacks, the other would shout out what was happening. By the time we got to the end of Season 6, we were dehydrated and probably insane. But the sense of achievement – Jesus. We felt like the two young lads from Cork who do all the rowing.

–Keep the eyes wide open and pull like a dog!

Anyway. There she is. Sitting in the dark, lit only by *Mad Men*. She gives me a quick glance but her eyes go straight back to Don.

–He's such a bollix, she says with more affection in her voice than I'd heard in – well, ever.

–Tell me honestly, I say. –What does he have that I don't have?

–Breaks for the ads, she says.

She puts Don on pause.

–Don't worry, Charlie, she says. –It's only telly.

But I'm not sure it's *only* anything. The box sets are consuming us. We're doing nothing else. I missed *Match of the Day* last Saturday because we couldn't get away from *The Leftovers*. I didn't even know it was Saturday.

I wish we could go back to the good old days, before videos and remote controls, when you had to wait till the following week to see what happened next. I loved *Colditz* when I was a kid but I could ignore it most of the time because it was only on on Thursdays. As for *Tenko*, I'd never have been able to live a normal life if it had been on more than once a week. All those women sweating away in a Japanese prisoner-of-war camp – nothing could have got me away from the telly.

Anyway, I'm thinking about doing a google, to see if there's an addiction counsellor in Dublin who can help wean us off Sky Box Sets, when something happens that helps me put the madness into perspective.

We go to her sister's house.

Simple as that.

But not that simple. We have to get away from our telly first. I give the remote control to one of the sons and tell him not to give it back to me till the next day, not even if I beg or threaten him, or try to bribe him. He's been through a bad *Sopranos* binge himself, and he missed the last World Cup and the birth of one of his kids, so he's sympathetic. He heads off to Liverpool for the weekend and takes the remote with him.

Anyway, we make it to Carmel's house. We're shaking a bit and the wife whimpers when she sees their telly. But we make it to their kitchen, and sit. She pats my hand under the table; I hold hers.

–It'll soon be over, I whisper.

She tries to smile.

But everyone's talking about bloody box sets. It's agony. We're like alcoholics at the bottle bank; we can smell the drink but there's none left.

I notice something. They're all trying to outdo each other; that's all it is. Naming a series they're hoping no one else has seen. Something Albanian, or a crime series from Greenland, hidden deep in the bowels of Netflix.

Then the wife pipes up – the first time she's spoken all night.

–Have yis seen *Bread and Adultery*? she says.

That shuts them all up. She taps my ankle with her foot; she's having them on, making it up.

–Who's in it? Carmel asks.

–Your man, says the wife. –You know – from that other one.

–Oh, says Carmel. –Him?

–And the girl from the ad.

–I think I've seen an episode of that, says someone else. –It looked brilliant.

The wife squeezes my hand. We'll be fine.

42

The wife says she wants to go to Dunkirk.

–What's wrong with Skerries? I ask her.

–You're gas, she says. –The film.

–The new one about the Allies landing in Normandy?

She stares at me.

–Charlie, she says.

–What?

She's still staring at me. But it's one of those concerned stares, like she's auditioning for a part in *Casualty*.

–Did you hear what you just said? she asks.

–I think so.

–You said *Dunkirk*'s about the Allied invasion.

–Yeah.

–You're the history buff, Charlie, she says. –You fall asleep every night with a book about the Second World War parked on your head.

It dawns on me while she's still speaking.

–Christ, I say. –Am I after mixing up Dunkirk with D-Day?

–I'm afraid so.

–Oh God.

I have to sit.

It's one of those terrifying moments. I was once in a car crash – or, nearly in a car crash, if that makes sense. The car ended up on the path, my heart was expanding, contracting, expanding, expanding, expanding. It was minutes before I knew what had happened. I'd nearly been killed – I'd very nearly died.

This is worse.

–It could happen to a bishop, says the wife.

–Fuck the bishop, I say. –It happened to me.

I look at her.

–I *know* what happened at Dunkirk, I tell her. –Blow by blow. I know it like the names of the kids. *Please, God,* I pray, *don't let her ask me to name the kids!*

–I know, she says.

–I know the difference between an invasion and – what's the opposite of an invasion?

–Evacuation? she says.

–Is that not what you do before a colonoscopy? I ask her.

She knows: I'm messing. We're back to normal.

But we're not. Well, I'm not. I need reassuring. I go through lists in my head, the dates of battles and surrenders. I manage to remember all the kids' names, and most of the grandkids, without resorting to Google. I look out the kitchen window and name all the dogs, and their breeds. *Rocky, half-poodle, half-boxer; Usain, half-dachshund, half-greyhound; Donald, half-schnauzer, half-gobshite.* I name them all and I'm feeling a bit better, a bit sturdier in myself, after a day or two.

And anyway, we go to *Dunkirk.* We go in on the bus.

–Over a million men died at the Somme.

–Charlie.

–What?

160

–You can stop now.

–Okay.

–You're grand.

–I know. Still a terrible loss of life, but.

The film is shattering. I haven't been to the pictures in ages but this is more like being on the Dunkirk beach, in the water, *under* the water. The things they can do with a camera these days, and the noise – I've never experienced anything like it. There's just a few moments when you can remind yourself that you're only at the pictures. That's whenever Kenneth Branagh's head is on the screen; neither of us can stand him.

He's up there now, talking shite, so I take a quick look around me.

I nudge the wife.

–There's no one snogging, I tell her.

–Jesus, Charlie, she says. –It's not a bloody rom com.

–We got off with each other during *The Exorcist*, I remind her. –I don't remember you objecting.

–That was different.

–How was it?

–Shut up, she hisses. –It wasn't a war film.

–We were wearing each other so much during *Full Metal Jacket*, we never found out who won the Vietnam War.

–Shut up!

Sir Kenneth is gone, so it's back to the chaos on the beach, in the air, and on the sea. At one point, she grabs my arm and doesn't let go.

She grabbed the wrong knee once. Years ago, during the first of the *Die Hard*s. She meant to grab mine, she told me, after she'd apologised to the lad on the other side of her – and his mott. We watched him limping out later, when the lights went up, but I don't know if he'd brought the limp in with him.

–You've maimed the poor chap for life, I told her.

–Count your blessings it wasn't you then, she said.
–Did you see the puss on his girlfriend, by the way.

That was the thing: going to the pictures was always a bit of gas. It didn't matter how serious it was, between the couples kissing, the noise of the sweet wrappers, and the curtain of cigarette smoke, you never forgot that it was a just a film.

This thing, though – *Dunkirk*. It's so real, so loud, so shocking, I'm surprised I'm not actually up to my neck in seawater. It's harrowing.

Your man from *Wolf Hall*, Mark Rylance, is up there on the screen. I know she likes him. She has that look – I've seen it when she's gazing at Don Draper from *Mad Men*.

I give her a nudge.

–It's not history you're watching now, sure it isn't?
–Shut up.

43

I'm a bit of a lost soul. So the wife is saying, anyway. I think she's just a bit sick of me moping around the place, especially in the evenings. She puts her head on my shoulder when she says it, but it's still a bit hurtful. And, just as her head touches the side of my neck, her hand reaches out and she grabs the remote control off me.

She wants me out of the house.

And so do I.

She says it again.

–You're a bit of a lost soul these days, Charlie.

And she turns from Brighton v. Newcastle to *The Great British Bake Off*. Normally, I'd be up off the couch like a cat with a banger up its arse, and straight down to the pub. But I stay where I am. I grab hold of her iPad and I google 'lost soul'. I've been hearing the phrase all my life but, now that I'm one of them, I want to know exactly what it means.

So, I type in 'lost soul' and this is what I get back: 'A soul that is damned'.

And that sends me down to the local for the first time in ages. If I'm on my way to eternal damnation, I'll need a pint before the trip.

And that's the problem. Walking to the local has become a short stroll to a possible hell. *Will he be there, will he be there?* My pal, Martin, has become as rare as a Leitrim man in Croke Park, and I hate drinking alone. Even just the one slow pint – I hate it.

Martin has fallen in love. He admitted it, himself, the last time we met.

–I heard *Puppy Love* on the radio this morning, he told me. –And I started crying. I couldn't help it.

–Donny Osmond?

He nodded.

–The song spoke to me, he said.

–Martin, I remind him. –You're over sixty.

–I know.

–You've enough grandkids to play against Bayern Munich.

–I know.

–With subs.

–I fuckin' know.

He sighed.

–It makes no sense, he admitted. –But––.

He took a slug from his pint and started singing.

–*I hope and I pray that maybe some day* –

–Martin, stop––.

–*You'll be back in my arms once again*––.

–Jesus, Martin – please –.

He was pining for Eileen Pidgeon who was actually in *my* arms – for an hour or so, anyway – years and years ago, when Donny Osmond was bleating his way to the top of the charts.

–Has she left you? I asked him, and I tried not to sound too hopeful.

–No, said Martin. –But I love imagining she has.

His eyes filled.

164

–It makes me so happy, Charlie.

–Ah, Jesus.

I got out of there without finishing my pint. Well, that's not true. I finished the pint but I didn't enjoy it. I was belching all the way home.

And now, tonight, I'm walking towards two equally dreadful possibilities: Martin won't be there, and Martin will be there. He won't be there and I'll have to endure my own company. I'll sit up at the bar and text the grandkids and hope they text me back, so I can keep my head down and look busy. Or, he will be there and I'll have to endure his lovesick elderly teenager routine.

He's there.

He's alone.

He's not wearing the Tommy Hilfiger jumper Eileen Pidgeon got him for his birthday.

So far, so good.

The jumper's pink, by the way, and way too small for him. It makes him look like a sausage before it hits the pan.

Anyway.

–Alright?

–Good man, says Martin.

He lifts a finger and the barman, Jerzy, sees him. He puts a glass under the Guinness tap and starts doing his job. Jerzy's from Poland and the lads from the football club started calling him Away Jerzy – or just Away. And now everyone does, including his wife and kids.

Anyway.

–How are things? I ask Martin.

Is he going to sing? Or cry? I'm all set to run – well, walk – if I have to.

–Grand, he says.

Is there a nicer, more reassuring word in the English language? Especially the way we use it in Ireland. It covers everything – the weather, your health, global politics, the quality of the pint in front of you, the points your granddaughter got in her Junior Cert. It covers – it hides – everything, including reality, what's right in front of your eyes. There could be a chap holding his scalp in his hand, blood pouring over his eyes, but if he tells you he's grand, it's official: he's grand. Leave him alone and move on – quick.

Martin doesn't look grand. He looks wretched; his skin's a strange grey colour. I'm guessing *Puppy Love* isn't speaking to him any more.

But he said he's grand, and I'm thrilled.

44

It's coming up to Halloween, so me and the wife are doing the rounds. Looking for drugs.

To sedate the dogs. And ourselves.

We always leave it too late. The first of the fireworks goes off in early September, always in broad daylight – some twit who can't wait for Halloween or even night time – and we hear the dogs going mad out the back. They're throwing themselves at the back door; they're howling at the moon that isn't out yet. It's not a great sound; there's nothing funny about it.

–I'll go down to the vet in the morning, I say.

And I always forget about it, because there isn't another rocket or banger attack for weeks, sometimes well into October.

This year it's been very quiet. I hear one cartwheel in mid-October, in the far distance.

–That'll be the North Koreans.

–You're gas.

I'm starting to wonder if there are any kids left in the neighbourhood, or if kids still go in to Moore Street to get their bangers.

It was one of the great signs of maturity when I was a kid: the walk down Moore Street and if one of the women asked you if you were looking for bangers, you were elected. You were grown-up, a bona fide teenager, ordained by the women on Moore Street.

Five years later, I walked down Moore Street again, hoping the women would ignore me. I was too old for bangers. I had an adult smell and hair on some of my face. I had a job, kind of a girlfriend, and a Honda 50. I carried the crash helmet, my adult credentials tucked under my arm. I'd nearly made it to the corner of Parnell Street when I heard the inevitable voice.

–Are you looking for bangers, love?

That was it, official: I was a kid for at least another year.

But, anyway. Last night, it was like a scene from *Apocalypse Now*. The poor oul' dogs were going berserk. Even I started howling.

So, this morning, I go down to the vet for canine sedatives, or whatever. But he won't believe the amount of dogs we have; he thinks I want to poison a horse or something. I phone the wife, to get her to verify the number. But he won't believe her either. It doesn't help that she doesn't actually know the precise number herself, and the dogs won't stay still long enough for her to count them.

Anyway, he gives me one tablet – one! – that looks like it wouldn't sedate a squirrel, let alone calm down a herd of enthusiastic dogs. So, we're doing the rounds of the neighbours, family and friends, taking any drugs they're not using. Painkillers, sedatives, anti-psychotics – we're not fussy. We accept them all gratefully. We'll mash them up and put them in with the food, with a few spoons of Benylin, for taste.

We keep most of the Benylin for ourselves, for Halloween night itself. It goes down very well with gin, by the way. A Hendrick's and Benylin – why wouldn't you?

Anyway. We're all set. The neighbours and family have been brilliant. We've enough drugs to floor the cast of *101 Dalmatians*.

But we're careful. We won't be giving the dogs any old thing. We want happy dogs, not catatonic dogs. We had a major scare a few years back when one of the neighbours, a desperate oul' hippie called Zeus – a nice enough chap, but Jesus. Anyway, Zeus gave us a Super-Valu bag full of mushrooms.

–Picked them myself, he told me. –On Fairyhouse Racecourse.

–And they'll do the trick, Zeus, yeah?

–Ah, man, he said. –I'm Exhibit A.

So, fair enough. I brought the mushrooms home and we fed them to the dogs, by the handful. The dogs are never that keen on vegetables, or anything that didn't once have legs on it. But they loved these yokes. They golloped them up, and not a squeak out of them for half an hour or so.

But then. Have you ever heard a gang of dogs singing *Love Will Tear Us Apart*? That was what we thought we heard. We ran out the back and the dogs – well, they weren't dogs any more. They were swimming, or trying to. Or they were flapping their front paws, trying to take off. They were talking Chinese to each other, or it might have been fluent Cork. Anyway, whatever it was, there wasn't one of them behaving like a dog, barking at the sky, pawing at the ground. The weirdest thing: they weren't wagging their tails.

I legged it down to Zeus.

–They were for you, man, he said. –Not the fuckin' dogs.

–Oh.

We'd left a few of the mushrooms in the bag, so myself and the wife took them, and we went outside and joined the dogs. And we came back in in plenty of time for Christmas.

45

I'm in an off-licence with one of my sons.

Lovely, says you. It's a day out with one of the children, kind of an adult version of a trip to the zoo. And it *is* lovely – any excuse to be with the kids, especially since they've grown up and left. Except it's dragging on a bit.

I said *an* off-licence, not *the* off-licence. *The* off-licence is only up the road, tucked in between the Spar and the Hickey's, and it has anything I'd ever be interested in drinking. But, so far, myself and the son have been in four different off-licences and I'm beginning to wonder if I should have brought a change of clothes and my passport.

The son is into the craft beer.

And fair enough – we all need a hobby. But he's taking it a bit far, I think. He has a book about it.

A book about beer! As far as I'm concerned, that's about as useful as a book about inhaling and exhaling – *Breathing for Dummies*. But I say nothing. I'm just glad to be with him. He asked me to come along, so I'm both delighted and bored out of my tree, at the exact same time.

Anyway. There's a beer he's fond of called Handsome Jack, and it's made in Kilbarrack. There's a brewery in Kilbarrack!

–Jaysis, son, I haven't had an education like this since I was thrown out of school.

I wasn't expelled from school, or anywhere else. But I like to pretend I was. It makes me more interesting, somehow; a bit wild and hard. And I just like making up stories. I once told the daughter I was in charge of Patrick Pearse's rifle in the GPO, in 1916. She seemed impressed – 'Really, like?' Then she asked me if I'd slipped down to Supermac's during a lull in the bombardment. It took me a while to cop on that she knew I was acting the maggot. She was ten.

Anyway, the brewery is in the Howth Junction industrial estate, in behind the GAA club there. So, our first stop is McHugh's on Kilbarrack Road, because – it says in the son's book – some beers don't travel well, so it might be 'a fun idea to try a glass in close proximity to the point of manufacture'. McHugh's is a stone's throw – a bottle's throw – from Howth Junction, so in we go.

And he buys a bottle.

One bottle.

There's two of us in the bloody car.

–Should we drink it now, son? I ask him.

We're back in the car with the bottle.

–Why? he asks.

–Well, I say. –We're in close proximity to the point of manufacture.

–Ah, no, he says. –The house is only a mile away.

–That's still in close enough proximity, is it?

–Ah, yeah.

–Fair enough.

It's a long day. There's a new beer, an IPA—

–What's that? I ask him.

–India Pale Ale.

I think I remember Ena Sharples from *Coronation Street* liking a half of pale ale, back in the days when the telly was black and white. But I say nothing.

Anyway, this new beer is called Howling Wreckage. It's from some mad brewery in the north of England, somewhere, and we spend the afternoon looking for it.

I don't really get it, all the craft beer. Guinness is crafty enough for me. When I was a kid, a teenager, me and my pals just wanted to become the men who drank Guinness. I remember my first pint, and being proud and slightly terrified. I wouldn't be able for it. I'd pass out or vomit, or I'd hate it – I'd look like a kid among the men. But, luckily, I liked it – or, I persuaded myself that I liked it – and it's been my poison ever since.

The beer you choose is like a marriage. Like your football team or your wife, you're stuck with it for life. Through triumphs and childbirth, relegation and the menopause, your team is your team, your wife is your wife, and your pint is your pint. Call me old-fashioned, I don't give a bollix.

We're in off-licence no.6. It's in Castleknock; we had to drive right through the Phoenix Park to get here. I've brought my reading glasses, because I can't make out half the stuff that's on the labels. I'm actually look-ing at the variety of crisps when I hear a shout.

–Yes!

It's the son.

–Found it!

He's holding a bottle of Howling Wreckage. It hits me; it's his face. It's the exact same expression he had

173

when he found the Buzz Lightyear that Santy had left for him at the end of the bed. It's my son there with the bottle; it's my little boy.

I know: there's a big difference between craft beer and *Toy Story* but, actually, it's the same buzz.

46

I get to the door of the local.

But I hesitate.

I'm a man on a mission.

Don't get me wrong now – I don't fancy myself as Tom Cruise in the *Mission Impossible*s. I wouldn't get a part in *Mission Possible*, or even *Mission Quite Straightforward*. But I'm going in there and not for a pint – or, not just for a pint.

It's quiet. Maybe ominous. Or maybe just empty.

I push open the door.

And it's the usual gang, dispersed around the shop. It's pub policy: the under-forties are barred, or at least discouraged. It's very clever, actually – something discreet about the decor and the clientele. Walk into my local and you just want to lie down and die. And if that's how you feel before you get there, it's like walking right into your natural habitat, the room of your dreams.

Anyway. The place is just quiet. I'd never really noticed it before – all the punters are staring at their phones. There's only two lads talking and they're leaning into each other, whispering like they're in a library.

There's a round table with four men at it. They've known one another for more than thirty years but they're all holding their phones right up to their faces. They're all half-blind and one of them has actually taken off his glasses so he can read what's on the screen.

Maybe they've run out of things to talk about. Maybe they're looking for the name of the footballer whose name they can't remember. Maybe it's just a break in the conversation. But I don't think so. I think it's an indication of something profoundly wrong about the way we live now. Because a woman walks past and not one of them looks up to have a gawk at her.

I know the woman.

It's Eileen Pidgeon.

–Ah, Charlie, she says. –How's yourself?

–Not too bad, Eileen. How's the hip?

In case you're thinking, 'Oh, good Jesus, he's having a fling with Eileen Pidgeon', I'm not. I'm not even dreaming about it. Well, I'm not dreaming *seriously* about it.

Eileen phoned me this morning. But she was using my pal Martin's phone. So, when I put my phone to my ear and heard, 'Charlie?', I thought Martin was after having the sex change – the hormone injections or whatever's involved.

Martin told me a while back that he identified as a woman, so I'm always a bit surprised when he turns up to the pub in the same jeans and jumper he's been wearing since the Yanks were hoisted out of Saigon.

Anyway.

–Martin, I said. –You cut the oul' balls off – good man.

–It's Eileen.

–Sorry?

–Eileen, she said. –Pidgeon. I'm using Martin's phone.

I believed her. I also wanted to climb into the washing machine and shut the roundy door.

–He doesn't know, she said.

–Sorry – what?

Now it was me who was sounding like the man who'd been having the hormone injections.

–I thought if I used my own phone, you wouldn't answer me, she said.

I coughed, and got a bit of the masculinity back up from my stomach.

–Why wouldn't I answer you? I asked.

–Well, she said. –I know. We have history.

I wasn't that pushed about history in school. But the way Eileen says 'history', the way the word slides into my ear, I want to run all the way in to Trinity College and sign up for a fuckin' Master's.

Anyway.

She wanted to meet me.

–For a chat.

–What, about Martin? I ask.

–Never mind Martin, she says.

Martin and Eileen have been doing a line since I kind of accidentally introduced them to each other. He's a widower who wishes he was a woman and she's a widow who seemed to think she'd met her ideal partner – some kind of a male lesbian. I'm trying not to sound bitter – but Eileen Pidgeon has been sitting in a little corner of my mind since I was sixteen, since the first and the last time she kissed me.

Anyway. Here I am. Nearly half a century later, and Eileen Pidgeon is standing right in front of me.

–Why are we here, Eileen? I ask her.

It sounds like a line from a film, even if I don't sound like the actor who should be delivering it.

–We'll have a drink first, Charlie, she says.

And fair enough; I'm forgetting my manners.

–Where's Martin? I ask her.

–He's at home with his football, she says.

–Does he know you're here?

–No.

Oh – Jesus.

–So, I say. –Why are we here?

My heart is in my head; I'm sure the whole pub can hear it.

–I want to talk to you about Martin, she says.

She puts her hand on my arn.

–I love him so much, Charlie.

Ah, Jaysis.

47

The daughter's an amazing young one, really.

I mean, all the kids and grandkids are amazing. It's the only proper way to look at them.

I remember years ago, one of the sons broke one of the neighbour's windows. The neighbour, Typhoid Mary, came charging in and she walloped me with her zimmer when I opened the door. I sorted the glass and put it in, myself. I was up on the ladder; it was a godawful windy day; I was hoping the putty would be as handy to use as it looked; and I was trying not to look too carefully into Mary's bathroom, especially at the seal in the bath – I swear to God – staring back out at me. But all I could think was, 'Jesus, that child's aim is brilliant.'

Another time, another of the sons came in from school and told us he'd failed an exam.

–How come? I asked him.

–It was stupid, he said.

It was the way he said it: I knew he was right. The exam *was* stupid and I gave him fifty pence for failing.

So. All my life I've tried, like the song, to accentuate the positive and eliminate the negative. And when it comes to the family I've never had to try. It's official: everyone belonging to Charlie Savage is brilliant.

Anyway.

Then there's the daughter. 'Brilliant' doesn't capture that young one; it doesn't come near. And I don't think it's because she's the youngest and the only girl, after a rake of boys.

–How many boys is it we have?

–You're gas.

–I'm serious.

–Four, Charlie. We have four sons.

–Thanks.

I am the father of four sons – four men. That fact fills my chest. It's as if the boys are my vital organs – my heart, my lungs, my kidneys, and the rest. Don't ask me which boy is which organ. I don't mean it literally and it's not a conversation I'd ever want to hear myself having, even on my deathbed.

–Which organ am I, Da?

–The bladder, son. You're the bladder. And I'll tell you something – you never let me down.

I suppose what I mean is, I can't imagine existing if I didn't have my children and grandchildren. In order of importance, I'd define myself as a father, a man, a Man United supporter, a SuperValu loyalty card holder, and a husband. I'm messing about the loyalty card but I'm dead serious about being a father. It's the biggest part of me.

I felt that way long before the daughter arrived. The boys all had their place in behind my ribcage. So, where is she?

She's right behind my eyes.

When I was a kid, I read all the comics – me and the brothers did. *The Beano, The Dandy, Sparky, Valiant* and *The Hotspur*. We read them all, over and over. Especially in the bed, when we were supposed to be going asleep. We'd be reading in the dark and thumping one another – that *is* possible when you're ten.

I remember my father's voice coming up at us through the floor.

–If I have to go up there, I'll Desperate Dan yis!

We were in stitches, biting our own arms so we wouldn't laugh too loud.

But, anyway. There was one cartoon called The Numskulls – I think it was in *The Beezer*. It was about these little lads, the numskulls, who lived inside the heads of people and controlled the different compartments of their brains.

That's the daughter – although she's no numskull. But she's always been behind my eyes.

I remember the first time she puked on my shoulder.

–Ah now, will you look at that!

–Calm down, Charlie, said the wife. –It's only vomit.

–I know, I said. –But it's so precise.

I had to shut my eyes and keep them shut – I felt so proud, so emotional, so stupid. It was the first time I'd cried at vomit that wasn't my own.

The baby looked up at me with a face that said, 'Deal with that.' And I did, happily.

She got right in behind my eyes and she's been steering me ever since. Or, more accurately, I look at the world through her eyes – or, I try to.

There's a woman on the radio. She's going on about sexual harassment, and she says something about 'unwanted attention' from men.

I come from a line of men who shout at the radio, and I shout now.

–Some of those wagons should be delighted with the unwanted attention.

The daughter is in the kitchen. And she looks at me. And she looks at me. And she looks at me.

I speak first.

–I'm wrong, I say.

She nods.

I know I'm wrong. I know it, I feel it.

–Sorry.

She shrugs, and walks out.

The wife is looking at me. She's grinning.

–What?

–Nothing.

48

They're all in the house, the wife's family. Her sister, Carmel, and the other sister, Dympna; Carmel's husband, Paddy, and Dympna's new partner whose name I won't bother remembering unless I meet him at least three more times.

Anyway. There we are. Sitting around the kitchen table, chatting away, having the crack. The food's been gobbled, the plates are in the dishwasher, the wife is taking the plastic off the After Eights.

And Carmel is staring at me.

–What? I say.

She doesn't answer, but she nudges the wife.

–Come here, she says. –Isn't Charlie a ringer for Dad?

Then they're all staring at me, the three sisters – and Paddy.

–What? I say again.

I seem to be asking that question on the hour, every hour, these days – and it's doing me no good. Because the more I ask the question, the less I'm finding out. But I can't help myself.

–What?

It's not really a question at all. It's more a cry for help.

183

Anyway, they're still staring at me, the sisters. Paddy, the bastard, is grinning away. Dympna's chap is demolishing the After Eights, three at a time. I don't think we'll be meeting him again.

–My God, says the wife. –You might be right, Carmel.

–Yeah, Dympna agrees. –The same head, like.

She's passing her phone around; there must be a snap of their da on the screen.

Paddy sits up.

–Could be worse, girls, he says. –He could be a ringer for your ma.

I take my line from the daughter; she has me very well trained.

–You can't say that, I tell him.

–Why not?

–Well, first of all, I tell him. –They're not girls, they're women. Second of all, your comment is totally sexist and unacceptable. And, third of all – fuck off and don't annoy me.

None of the women congratulate me. I don't think they're even listening. The wife looks a bit pale; she's staring at the screen, at me, at the screen. Carmel looks a bit confused. Dympna is looking at the black chocolate on the tip of her boyfriend's nose.

I have to escape before they decide that I actually am my wife's father.

–The jacks, I say.

And I stand up.

–I'll be back in a minute, I say, although I'm not sure I mean it. I want to get out of the room, out of the house. I want to emigrate.

But I compromise and just head up to the bathroom. It's becoming my favourite room. I get in there and I stare in the mirror, at myself.

184

The father-in-law is long dead and I can't really remember what he looked like. I remember his voice – because there was a lot of it. The man would whisper in Dublin and flocks of flamingos would take flight, in Kenya.

I keep looking in the mirror.

I seem to be spending a lot of time doing that these days, staring at myself. So the wife says.

–You're a bit long in the tooth for vanity, Charles, she said a few days ago.

–And you're much too old for sarcasm, I said back.

She was wrong: it wasn't vanity – it isn't vanity. It's science – I realise that now.

I go across to our bedroom. The wife keeps some old photos in the locker on her side of the bed. I hate rooting in there. It's none of my business and I'm always a bit terrified of what I'll find. Old love letters, *new* love letters, a flick knife, a moustache – the possibilities are endless and horrible. But I find what I want – a snap of her Da.

I bring it back to the jacks and I hold it up – I park it beside my face.

–My God, I whisper, and the flamingos in Kenya give their feathers a shake.

We're not exactly peas in the same pod, me and her da. But – there's no getting away from it – we're alike.

I'll be honest: I feel a bit sick. Was that what she was doing all those years ago, when she grabbed my shoulders, called me an eejit, and kissed me till my head was numb? Was she looking for a man who was going to become her father?

There's another photo that has other men in it besides her da. It's a wedding snap, a line of middle-aged men.

I see now: they all look the same. I've just become one of them. Paddy downstairs – he looks like them too.

That's my discovery: as we get older, we all become the same man. It's depressing but somehow reassuring. It's democratic, at least.

I think of all the women I know and have ever known, and they definitely don't become the same woman.

That's a relief.

I bounce down the stairs to tell them the news.

49

I check to make sure I have everything. I pat my pockets and recite the line my father delivered every time he was leaving the house.

–My spectacles, my testicles, my wallet and my watch.

–You're gas, says the wife.

She's smiling.

Because we're all set, me and the grandson. We're men on a mission and we're heading into town – for the Christmas clothes.

The Christmas clothes is a tradition that goes right back to the time when the Savages were savages. We had new clothes for Christmas centuries before Christ was even born. The shepherds in the stable were dressed in the rags they'd been wearing for years but one of them, Ezekiel Savage, was wearing a brand new jumper and slacks from the Bethlehem branch of Dunne's.

Anyway. It's just me and the grandson and we're getting the grandson's Christmas clobber, with no interference from women. Strictly speaking he doesn't need the clothes; the daughter has him dressed like Leo Varadkar, stripy socks and all. But it's tradition we're talking about here. The Savages, like half of Dublin, always had new clothes for midnight mass.

There was a chap in my class in school, Terence Halpin, and he wore the Christmas clothes into school after the holidays, and that was what he wore every day – *every* day – right through the year, until they fell off him. They were the only clothes he had. I remember once – I think we were in second year, in secondary school – he came in after the Christmas holidays wearing a yellow waistcoat. His mother had opted for the waistcoat instead of a jumper. The poor lad was freezing; it was early January. We gave him a terrible time. We called him Tweety, after the bird in the *Looney Tunes* cartoons. I'd apologise to Tweety – sorry, Terence – if I met him today.

I actually did meet him about forty years ago. He was with this gorgeous-looking young one.

–Howyeh, Tweety, I said.

I couldn't remember his real name.

–Fuck off, Shirley, he said back, but I'm betting he could remember *my* real name. His mott burst out laughing, and I came away feeling happy for him.

Kind of.

Anyway.

It was Shirley Temple, by the way. I had a head of hair that my mother loved and I detested, until I was old enough to shave it off and become Dublin's least frightening skinhead – and my mother didn't talk to me for seven years.

Anyway. The daughter has shown me pictures of some of the clothes she wants for the grandson, and the shops where I can get them – and the credit union where I can arrange the loan. But I ignore her. She wants him ready for *The X Factor*, but I want him ready for middle-age. He's getting jeans and a jumper. The jumper will be grey, black or blue.

Anyway. Here we go. His hand is in my hand. Down Talbot Street, across to Henry Street. I look at what he looks at; I stop when he stops. I'd forgotten that about kids: everything fascinates them. The Christmas lights are on but he's counting the cigarette butts on the path.

It takes us three days to get to the Spire. Well, an hour – it's a journey that would normally take five minutes. He doesn't notice the Spire when we get there. He's still looking at the ground.

So am I.

–There's one that's hardly been smoked, look!

But he's moved from butts to chewing gum. He won't budge off North Earl Street until he's counted every gob. His concentration is frightening; whoever keeps saying that the young have no attention span hasn't a clue. He ignores two dreadful choirs, three pissed Santys, four calling birds, and a gang of Italian tourists who seem to be trying to get the statue of James Joyce to talk back to them.

The day isn't going as planned but I don't think I've ever been happier.

Eventually – he stops.

–Hard 'ork, G'anda!

–How many was that, love?

–Un t'ousand, t'ee hundit and nixty–six!

–My God, I say. –You must be thirsty after all that, are you?

He nods, and he nods again.

–We'll go for a drink, so, I say. –But first we need to get you a drinking jumper.

He loves that.

–And d'inkin' t'ousers!

–Now we're talking. Drinking trousers.

So, off we go again, across O'Connell Street. And now, for the first time, he notices the lights.

I can feel it, from his hand to my hand – his delight, his excitement. I'm holding his hand but I'm holding all of my children's hands, and my ma's hand, and my da's. I'm holding more than sixty years of living and love, sadness and joy, regret and acceptance.

–What colour drinking jumper do you want, love?

–G'ey!

–Grey?

Ah Jesus, I'm starting to cry.

50

It's a year since I've seen the lads. It's always a bit hair-raising. Well, it is for me, because I still have stuff on my head that could reasonably be defined as hair. What I mean is, I'm always excited and I'm always a bit worried.

We meet once a year, us men who grew up together. We've been doing it for more than forty years, since we all started going our separate ways – when we left home, got bedsits, mortgages; met women, had kids; emigrated, came back; divorced, remarried, were widowed; had grandkids, great-grandkids; were made redundant, retired; got sick, recovered, or didn't recover. There used to be six of us. Now there are four. I think.

We're meeting where we always meet, in Mulligan's of Poolbeg Street. Unlike us, Mulligan's never changes. I can't see a thing that's different, except a few of the taps. But the Guinness tap is the one that matters, and it's exactly where I left it the last time I was in here. I point to it and the barman nods, like he sees me every day and not just once a year at Christmas.

I'm the first to arrive. I always am. I'm unusual; I'm never, ever late. I've always been like that. Back in the day when I went to mass, I'd turn up so early for the half-twelve mass that I was actually late for the half-eleven.

Anyway. The place is busy but there are a few empty stools at the counter. I'm not a big fan of the word 'perfect'. Everything seems to be bloody perfect these days. I handed the young one in the Spar a baguette and a can of beans this morning and she said, 'Perfect'. The little grandson showed me dog poo on his football boot, and *I* said, 'Perfect'. So, I warned myself to be vigilant – to ban 'perfect' from my armoury, unless the thing actually is perfect.

An empty stool in a full pub qualifies as perfect and I park my less than perfect arse on top of it. Mission accomplished – I've established a beachhead. And I don't have to wait too long for the rest of the Marines.

First in is Gerry.

He sees me.

–For fuck sake!

Joxer is right behind him.

He sees us.

–For fuck sake!

We're a gang of oul' lads but we're not closed to the lifestyle changes. We hug each other – something we would never have done even a few years back. We get our arms around one another.

–The state of yeh!

–Good to see you, man.

–Ugly as ever.

–Shag off now.

I get back up on my stool before it's kidnapped.

–Pints? I ask the lads.

–Good man.

–Lovely.

There's three of us now. We're waiting for Chester, although we say nothing. Chester lives in England – in Manchester – and he comes over just for the Christmas pints. He used to stay with his parents, then his ma, then one or other of his sisters. They're all gone now, so he stays the night in one of the hotels out near the airport. There's no one belonging to him still alive in Ireland. He doesn't have an email address; he doesn't do texting. I send him a postcard with the date and the time – every year.

–How's all the family?

–Grand. Yours?

–Grand, yeah – not too bad. Any more grandkids?

–One or two – maybe three.

–You lose track, don't yeh?

–I kind of do.

–Great pub.

–Smashing pub.

We say it every year. We feel at home here; we feel it's ours. The atmosphere is good but they don't overdo the Christmas shite – the decorations and that.

Still no sign of Chester. Still we say nothing.

We never talk about the old days but, still, they're there. We never talk about the schooldays – the mitching, the beatings, the crack, the mad Christian Brothers. We never talk about the girls we used to fancy – well, hardly ever. And one girl always gets a mention.

–D'yis remember Eileen Pidgeon?

–Oh, God – stop the lights.

I say nothing.

Still no sign of Chester.

We don't talk much about the past but we know: it's why we're here. It's why we hug, why we grin, why we put hands on shoulders. It's why we slag each other unmercifully, why we get serious when we talk about our kids.

Still no sign of—

–Ah – for fuck sake!

It's Chester. Fat and kind of magnificent, filling the door.

–My fuckin' flight was delayed.

–Ryanair?

–Fuckin' Luftwaffe, he says. –You could see the fuckin' bullet holes in the wings.

He's been out of the country for forty years but he still talks like he's from up the road. Which he is. Which we all are. And we're together again – like we've always been.

Perfect.

51

Pint?

It's the text I've been waiting for all day. I'm into my coat like Batman into his – whatever Batman jumps into when he's in a hurry. And I'm gone, out onto the street – through the letter box; I don't even open the door.

–Seeyis!

And I'm pawing at the pub door before I answer the text.

He's there already, alone. My buddy, Martin. And there's a pint sitting beside his, waiting for me.

It was Martin who texted me but, to be honest, after a week locked up in the house with the grandson's toys and the daughter's lectures, I'd have jumped at the chance if Mother Teresa had texted me. A few pints with Mother Teresa? Ah, the crack. I read somewhere that she was a Manchester City supporter. Although, now that I think of it, that might have been Liam Gallagher. He's a ringer for her when he has his hood up.

Anyway. It isn't Mother Teresa – or Liam Gallagher – who's waiting for me. It's Martin. And I'm glad.

We go back, me and Martin. Back to when I was a much younger man and I came in here one day for a slow pint, before I went home to tell the wife that I was out of work.

November the 8th, 1993.

I was sitting there on my own, wondering what I was going to tell her, how I was going to say it, what we'd tell the kids – trying to stay calm. Resisting the urge to have another pint, and another, and another. Failing.

–Another pint, please.

When Martin was suddenly beside me – or, I noticed him for the first time.

–Alright? he said.

–Yeah, I said. –Yeah – actually, no.

I didn't know him. I'd seen him at the side of the football pitch on Sunday mornings with the other fathers and mothers, watching our kids get mucky. I'd seen him coming and going around the place – but I'd never really spoken to him before.

–What's the story? he said.

–Ah, well, I said. –I've been let go off the job.

–Bad, he said.

–And I've to go home now and tell the wife.

–Bad.

–Yep.

–I don't fuckin' envy you.

He said nothing for a bit. Neither did I. I looked at my pint settling.

–I don't want to, I said then.

–What? he said.

–Go home.

–I know, he said. –But it has to be done.

–I know.

Again, we said nothing for a bit.

He broke the silence.

–I'll say this, just, he said. –If we'd been here like this a couple of years ago, I'd have been feeling really sorry for you – I'd have had nothing to say, really. Now, but—. There's work out there. You'll be grand.

He was right. I was back in work in a fortnight and I was never unemployed again. Then, there, sitting beside him – I don't know why – I just believed him.

He watched me finishing my pint.

–Seeyeh, he said.

I knew what he was doing: he was sending me home, to do what had to be done.

I stood up.

–Seeyeh, I said, and I went home.

I've thought about it since, that first time I spoke to Martin. He was like your man, Clarence, the angel in *It's a Wonderful Life*, when he persuades Jimmy Stewart that his life is worth living. I wasn't suicidal or anything; I wasn't getting ready to fling myself into the Liffey. But it was good having him there beside me, at that moment.

We watched that film five times over the Christmas. The daughter loves it and, I have to admit, so do I. Especially your woman, Donna Reed. I always end up wishing I was Jimmy Stewart running home in the snow.

And Martin looks quite like Clarence these days – the same nose and all.

We sit and say nothing. We're good at that. We're in no hurry. We're happy enough in the silence.

He speaks first.

He puts his pint back down on its mat.

–How was your year?

–Shite, I say.

–Same here, he says.

–You've had your ups this year, I remind him.

197

I'm thinking of Eileen Pidgeon. I'm thinking how unfair it is, that a Clarence-the-angel lookalike can have a torrid affair with the elderly woman of my dreams.

He doesn't disagree with me.

–It evens out, but, he says. –The good shite and the bad shite.

–It's all shite, I say. –Is that what you're saying?

I love a bit of philosophy.

–It is, he agrees.

–I'm with you.

We sit there, together. Like two men in a stationary lifeboat. We're going nowhere and we really don't need saving. We won't be wishing each other a Happy New Year. We don't do that stuff. But I'm glad he's here beside me.

52

I hate the new year. Actually, I hate everything new. Nearly everything. Clothes, music, recipes, neighbours – the list is probably endless. And the exceptions – babies and hips – they just prove the rule. The vast majority of new things are a pain in the arse, especially the new years.

I'm not suggesting that we shouldn't have a new year. I'm not stupid. I know that the earth orbits the sun and I accept that we have seasons and that your man, Shakespeare, was on the button when he said if winter comes, then spring is probably tagging along behind it.

Grand.

But it's the whole Year Zero thing that gets on my wick. Every 1st of January, we're expected to become new people.

We were out on the street at midnight on New Year's Eve. It's excruciating, having to shake hands with, and even hug, people I can't stand. But the wife makes me come out with her.

–Stop whingeing.

–I'm not whingeing.

–Here's your jacket – get up.

Anyway, one of the neighbours, Brendan, was hugging me – a bit half-heartedly, in my opinion. A half-hearted hug is even worse than a full-blooded one, I think.

Anyway.

–What are you giving up? he says.

–What?

–For the new year, he says. –What are you giving up?

–It's not bloody Lent, I tell him.

–Well, it's no more junk food for me, he says.

You should see the state of this chap. He looks like a greyhound that never caught up with the rabbit. I don't know what he sees in the mirror – because he's hardly there. I'm not sure I'm even talking to him in the dark. It might be just an optical illusion in a lemon-coloured jumper. Anyway, I never saw a man more in need of a couple of crisps – and he was giving them up. Because it was the 1st of January.

By the way, I saw him in the Spar yesterday and he was hovering close to the Pringles.

Anyway.

It wasn't always like this. There was a time when the only thing you expected from the new year was a hang-over. Now, though, we're expected to alter our bodies and – even worse – the way our minds operate.

I've been living with my mind – my brain, my personality, whatever you want to call it – for more than sixty years. And we've been getting along fine. There have been off-days and weeks and one godawful decade, but, generally speaking, me and the mind have managed to get this far without too much aggro or damage. If my mind suggests a pint, I'm often in agreement. If the mind gives me the nudge and tells me to say something nice to the wife, the timing is generally spot-on. And *what* I say to her – 'Your hair's nice', 'I'm with you, love – it's not fair', 'It's your brain I fell in love with, not your cooking' – the mind has usually delivered something apposite and even – once or twice – wise. And devious.

So, anyway. I'm content enough with my mind, in a happily miserable kind of way. The memory isn't what it used to be, but I can't blame the mind for that; we both decided not to bother with the fish and the crosswords. And what do we actually have to remember? A few names, our own name, our team, the colour of the front door, the difference between the dishwasher and the washing machine. That's about it. And my mind – I'm reluctant to call it my intellect – is well up to that.

Anyway. I'm happy enough with the mind I was given and I'll have no problem accepting its guidance, all the way up to my terminal breath. 'Keep the mouth shut there, Charlie – you'll be a better-looking corpse.' The body and the mind – we're in it together for the last stretch of the long haul.

But, no.

Apparently not.

Apparently, I've to become more optimistic.

–Your outlook's too bleak, like, says the daughter.

–Bleak doesn't cover it, love, says the wife. –He's windswept and desolate.

–So is the Wild Atlantic Way, I tell them. –And the tourists are flocking to it.

–Well, there's no one flocking to you, buster, says the wife. –The head on you.

–What's wrong with my head?

–New year, new man, Dad, says the daughter. –You should start giving yourself daily done wells. Love yourself, like. What did you do well today?

–Oh sweet Jesus, I say, and I leg it up to the bed. And I congratulate myself as I climb in.

–Well fuckin' done, Charlie.

The wife gets in a few hours after me.

–Come here, I say. –You don't want me to change, do you?

I wait.

–Do you?

She puts her hand on my back and pats it.

That's a No. I'm safe for another year.